"You're coming with me," Gunnar said.

"I'm not, Gunnar. I have a company to run. I don't even know where exactly you wish to take me."

"Iceland. There we will deal with your perfidy, and once we discover whether or not you're carrying my baby, you will be treated accordingly."

"And how is that?" Her voice felt scratchy and dry.

"Olive, if the child you carry is mine, there is no question of what will happen next. If you are having my heir, you will be my wife."

Millie Adams has always loved books. She considers herself a mix of Anne Shirley (loquacious but charming and willing to break a slate over a boy's head if need be) and Charlotte Doyle (a lady at heart but with the spirit to become a mutineer should the occasion arise). Millie lives in a small house on the edge of the woods, which she finds allows her to escape in the way she loves best— in the pages of a book. She loves intense alpha heroes and the women who dare to go toe-to-toe with them (or break a slate over their heads).

Books by Millie Adams

Harlequin Presents

His Secretly Pregnant Cinderella

The Kings of California

The Scandal Behind the Italian's Wedding
Stealing the Promised Princess
Crowning His Innocent Assistant
The Only King to Claim Her

Visit the Author Profile page
at Harlequin.com for more titles.

Millie Adams

THE BILLIONAIRE'S BABY NEGOTIATION

HARLEQUIN®
PRESENTS™

Recycling programs
for this product may
not exist in your area.

ISBN-13: 978-1-335-73854-7

The Billionaire's Baby Negotiation

Copyright © 2022 by Millie Adams

For questions and comments about the quality of this book,
please contact us at CustomerService@Harlequin.com.

Harlequin Enterprises ULC
22 Adelaide St. West, 41st Floor
Toronto, Ontario M5H 4E3, Canada
www.Harlequin.com

Printed in U.S.A.

THE BILLIONAIRE'S
BABY NEGOTIATION

CHAPTER ONE

THERE MUST BE a German word for that near unendurable feeling of wanting to punch someone and make out with them at the same time.

At least, Olive Monroe felt there *should* be. She had a passable understanding of German and had never heard that word though. Neither was it in English, Japanese, Chinese or any of the other languages she'd learned to foster her career in business.

It was what she felt every time she looked at Gunnar Magnusson.

Billionaire, philanthropist, possibly part-time Viking, and full-time pain in her ass from the first moment she could remember.

Gunnar being an impediment was an early childhood memory.

The first time she'd seen him, she'd been six, he'd been sixteen.

Their fathers had been locked in competitive negotiations, and she'd been sitting outside on a bench, just outside the conference room. There had been a spread of goodies on the table, and her father had warned her not to touch anything. But she was certain it did not include a chocolate cupcake that were sitting out there for anyone to take.

But just as she'd steeled up her confidence to take it, a tall, blond man had walked into the room—at the time she'd thought he was a man—and had eaten the cupcake in one bite.

He'd turned and looked at her then and there had been something like embarrassment in his blue eyes, which had quickly turned to haughty disdain.

It was later she would find out that he was the only son of her father's greatest business rival.

Gunnar Magnusson, son of Magnus Ragnarson, the most hated man in the Monroe household. And he had eaten her cupcake.

It had been a *very* disappointing birthday.

It could be argued perhaps that her father had contributed at least in some part to the disappointment of the birthday, given that she had spent it sitting outside of his tense negotiations.

Her mother had died when Olive was only a baby, the love of her father's life, gone. And rather than leave her with nannies, he had taken her into his world. He had never acted like she should be a boy, or like he would have been better off without her. He treated her like she was an integral part of this world—his company, which had been his one true love before meeting her mother, before having her.

She knew he didn't mean to give her a bad birthday. He meant to give her a birthday with him. And he had taken her for sushi after, so that had been nice.

Her father was all she had. If she felt disappointment about not having a birthday party with other children, a pretty cake and pony rides, it didn't matter. It was easier to make Gunnar the bad object.

It wasn't as if he took any great care to avoid irritating her. No. They had clashed constantly over the years.

It was the trouble of their fathers being in the same industry. Constantly competing for the same tech contracts.

There had been a space of time when she'd had some relief from Gunnar. When he'd been eighteen he'd gone off on his own and started his own corporation in manufacturing and had been absent from her sphere other than industry events, which he'd often come to, dressed in tuxedos and wreaking havoc on her sanity.

She could remember—vividly—the time she'd been fifteen and he'd showed up at a charity event. He'd walked into the highly polished hotel and everything had seemed to stop.

Most men looked tamed in a tuxedo. It was the fashion of the sleek and sophisticated. But Gunnar, all broad shoulders, chest and muscular arms, slim waist and hips, looked all the more dangerous.

And Olive had fallen into a potted plant.

To her horror, it was Gunnar who appeared to lift her out, his large, warm hand, so rough and masculine, wrapping itself entirely around hers and making her feel small and fragile. Red, and hot.

Very like he had eaten her cupcake all over again, except there was something different too.

She was not fifteen now, she knew what it was now.

She was just thankful fifteen-year-old Olive hadn't known, because the poor thing had already been overcome by shame at her graceless tumble into the greenery.

She hadn't needed to know she was experiencing sexual attraction for the first time in her life on top of everything else.

When she had been seventeen, Gunnar's father had died.

"We must go to the funeral, Olive."

She'd looked at her father in confusion. *"But you hated him."*

"He was my rival. Iron sharpens iron. Having him as an adversary made me better."

It was then she realized the complex nature of such relationships. And she'd been somewhat relieved. That maybe her feelings for Gunnar were something along those lines. Because it wasn't a rivalry where you wanted your enemy to die in a fire.

You needed an opponent to race against to be your fastest.

A skilled opponent was a good thing.

That was when Gunnar had assumed control of Magnum Enterprises. And he'd come back into her life in a much more regular space.

And her feelings for him had only grown more and more tangled. Because he was the one going into those meeting rooms, and she was still sitting outside.

"Someday," her father had said, *"you'll go toe-to-toe with him. And you'll win. Maybe you'll win."*

He'd smiled at her sadly.

"I don't think I have that kind of time. But you... you're a brilliant mind, Olive, and you can do it. But you must remember. Compete without mercy. Never let emotion cloud your judgment. Give no quarter."

She carried those words with her now. Because now she was the one who went into the boardroom. It was her battle now.

And Gunnar was her opponent.

They were the same. Locked in negotiations, all day every day sometimes, to secure the best and highest paying contracts.

But this... This was the big one. Her father's baby. The one he'd worked on for years, the one he'd died before finishing.

Getting their touchscreen system, their operating system, into the largest fleet of electric cars in the world, and it would bother him so much if she won.

Gunnar Magnusson had been a vanguard of green energy for years. And while Ambient was slightly behind on that, Olive was making up for lost time. Her father had been a stickler for tradition. For doing things the way they had always been done. Not that Magnus had been any different. It was only that Gunnar had taken over Magnum Enterprises a decade ago, and Olive had only been running Ambient six months, taking over her father's unfinished projects and working as hard as she could to fulfill his goals, to be what he'd trained her to be.

And if not for what had happened after her father's funeral, she wouldn't have felt at all guilty about the way in which she had gone about gaining her info for today's meeting.

It was a bit of corporate espionage. But this contract would see her business tied up for the next decade. Constantly innovating and pushing the new technology in green energy vehicles forward, and she wouldn't have to see Gunnar for... Well, it would at least be ten years.

Because she wouldn't be able to compete for another contract on this level with everything existing that she had. They had been playing a chess game for years. Magnum's technology was ubiquitous in the corporate world. Ambient was for artists. Ambient had the most successful phone.

Magnum provided the GUI and back-end software for most things that ran on computer chips. Including a massive contract with the largest airline to use their microchips to keep the planes in the sky.

It was all global domination, and the more computerized vehicles became... The more competitive that all was.

Anyway. Ambient was just better for something like that. It needed to be slick, visuals based and artistic. Clean. In her opinion, everything that Magnum did was dull. It was corporate. And it showed.

But she would save that for the pitch, rather than hyping herself up on her own achievements in the corridor.

Twenty minutes until the meeting. And her mouth was watering.

Because she wanted a chocolate cupcake.

Damn him.

This was why she needed distance. Her father might have been able to see Magnus as iron sharpening his iron, but Gunnar wasn't iron for her. He didn't make her sharp.

He made her soft.

She'd done this to prove it didn't have to be that way. Done it to be who her dad had raised her to be.

She needed to be iron.

She couldn't do that with Gunnar around her all the time.

And just then, she heard heavy footsteps in the corridor. And looked. And there he was, striding toward her in a navy-blue suit custom-fit to conform to his hulkingly masculine figure. He was large, blond, with a beard and piercing blue eyes that she was certain could see right beneath her black turtleneck.

She didn't do suits.

"Little Olive," he said. "How nice to see you."

As he always called her.

He'd said it at her father's funeral too.

"Little Olive. How are you?"

And it had broken her. To see him, not in a business meeting, not in a highly visible charity event. But in the quiet after the funeral. With his blue eyes different than she'd ever seen them. They didn't hold a challenge.

There was concern.

And she'd wept.

And he'd held her.

She hardened herself against that memory now.

"Hello, Gunnar. Not raiding any villages and carting women off against their will today?"

He arched a pale brow. "The pillaging must cease sometimes."

"Must it? For here you are."

"Is it pillaging, or is it business? I know you like to pretend to be very victimized by needing to compete with the best."

"But see, I win half the time. So I'm not certain how you can maintain that you're the best."

"Because some people prefer form over function."

"No. It's just that some companies are capable of providing both. Some of us think outside the suit," she said, taking a step toward him and tugging the lapel of his jacket. She regretted it in an instant. Heat arced between them.

And she tried, she really tried, to remember the times they'd clashed over the years. Not the time he'd pulled her out of the potted plant.

Not the time he'd taken her back to her empty family home after that very worst day of her life, when she'd said goodbye to her father and felt more alone than ever.

Not when he'd sat across from her in that living room and looked at her with sympathy. Let her cry and talk and share memories. Had wrapped her in a blanket and carried her upstairs.

And when he'd set her down in front of her bedroom door, all disheveled and her eyes stinging from tears, she'd put her hand on his chest and felt his heart beating hard.

He'd taken his jacket off downstairs and was wearing just a white shirt, unbuttoned at the throat and she'd wanted him.

She wasn't fifteen and she knew how she wanted him now.

So she'd stretched up on her toes, her mouth a breath from his.

"No, Olive."

The refusal stung, even now.

"Go to sleep. You're tired and grieving. And you would not thank me in the morning."

He'd hurt her. Broken her with that refusal, even as he'd knit her emotions together with his concern earlier.

And when she'd seen him again at a business function he'd acted as if the night hadn't happened.

She'd been outraged and relieved all at once.

Outraged she was still affected by him. Relieved he wasn't going to humiliate her by bringing up her attempt at kissing him.

But sadly, she still wasn't cured. Which had fueled her need to win this contract. It now held the weight of so many of her needs.

To see her father's dreams come to fruition. To be as strong and ruthless as he'd wanted her to be.

To get Gunnar out of her life so she could be free of this tangle of feelings.

Because even now there was heat. All these months there had been heat.

For far longer than that. For years, her late-night fantasies were of being carried away by a Viking and tied up as his prisoner in his longhouse…

Well. No one had to know that. And no one ever needed to see her stack of medieval Viking romance novels.

There was a particularly interesting Caitlin Crews on the subject that had occupied the last few nights.

It was probably *not* the best reading material just before heading in to see Gunnar. But being totally truthful, it didn't matter if she read the books just before seeing him or not. He owned that part of her. He was tangled up in so many things. In formative ideas about fantasy, sex and romance.

It was easy for her to tell herself she'd never had a romantic life because she'd been so busy training to take over Ambient.

But the truth was a lot more specific. A lot more Icelandic.

A lot more…him.

"Very avant-garde. Nobody has ever done this…" He gestured over her outfit. "I have simply never seen it."

"I'm not trying to be *original*, I'm trying not to take up my time with ridiculous details that have nothing to do with innovation."

"I brought you something."

She knew that he had. He reached into his briefcase, and pulled out a chocolate cupcake. Oh, she despised him. Because it was like Pavlov's dog, and she had a feeling that he knew it.

He had taken to bringing her a chocolate cupcake at each and every one of these pitch meetings. Which only became more and more heated.

They never spoke to the person whose contract they were competing for separately. No. They always did it together. Their fights over who would win these wars had become legendary, and people wanted a front row seat.

He claimed, and she did not believe him, that the cupcake was a peace offering. She thought that it was just to make her angry. But the problem was, she was now conditioned to need a chocolate cupcake prior to these events.

And if she refused, she felt that he would know it.

"Thank you," she said taking the cupcake in hand.

Her stomach growled. And she just grinned past it. She began to delicately lick at the frosting, and when she looked up, she saw that there was heat in his blue eyes.

Yes. This was not one-sided.

"You know. Whoever wins this contract will be tied up for so long… I daresay we won't be seeing each other for quite some time."

"Indeed," he said.

She twirled the cupcake in a circle as she licked at the chocolate butter cream. Making eye contact with him. "I'll miss you. Or maybe I'll just miss the cupcakes."

"I'll get you a subscription to a bakery service. Cake of the month."

She put her hand on her chest and looked at him with what she hoped was mournful sadness. "That would help ease the pain."

"What will be next for you," she said, "when you

don't get this contract? Will you fade off into the distance and focus all of your attention on your other endeavors?"

"I won't lose," he said.

"Oh, Gunnar. You are going to lose. You're gonna lose bad." She smiled at him.

He curled his upper lip, almost as if in a sneer, and then tapped his blindingly white front tooth. "You have chocolate. Just there."

"Of course I do, dumbass," she said, closing her mouth and running her tongue quickly along her teeth. "I'm eating a chocolate cupcake."

"Still. You might want to sort that out before the meeting starts."

"I'll just be a moment."

She stopped in the bathroom and made sure that everything with her teeth looked good, and by the time she was finished it was time to step into the meeting.

Poor Gunnar. She almost felt sorry for him. Because she had seen his entire presentation. Months ago. And she had tailored her projected technology accordingly. He would simply never know what hit him.

And being so confident in her position allowed her to sit back during his presentation and focus on his hands. The way they caressed the different visuals. The prototypes. The sharpness in his consonants, the masculine set of his broad shoulders… Yes. It was so easy to imagine him as a Viking marauder.

She really didn't understand how you can hate a person so much, and also have that same person exclusively be the one man you ever wanted to go to bed with. Olive wasn't a prude. Her reading material proved that.

But she was busy, and she had decided a long time ago that there was no point pursuing anything with a man who didn't make her half as excited as a new piece of technology… Or Gunnar Magnusson.

Because if a man she disliked could make her entire body ache in inappropriate places… A man she liked should be able to do just as much with one look. And she had never felt compelled to experiment physically. She had kissed a couple of men. And again, the issue was that one withering glare from Gunnar gave her weeks more fantasy fodder than any of those kisses had.

That moment in the hall at her family home…when she'd been able to breathe him in, when she'd been so close to him she could feel his heat…

It haunted her, even now as they pretended that evening of tenderness, of connection had never happened, it haunted her.

So what was the point?

What was the point.

If she couldn't get away from him, there would never be anyone else.

Not ever.

And Gunnar was finished. And it was her turn.

"Thank you. That was very interesting, Mr. Magnusson. I think, though, Mr. Yamamoto, that you will find this to be the most compelling direction." And she laid out a thorough a assassination for Gunnar's system. She had identified every flaw in his design, and she had tweaked and reflected her own in response. She had set about making a system that annihilated his. And in her—not her words, but profiles that had been done on her—engaging and down-to-earth style that made technology so accessible anyone could understand, she laid out her plan for the fleet.

And in the end, she was the one who got the handshake.

"Congratulations, Miss Monroe. Ambient is the clear choice to be fulfilling the need for our fleet."

Gunnar didn't react. This wasn't the first time he had lost to her. But it was his biggest loss. He shook Mr. Yamamoto's hand gamely, and smiled. "Perhaps we could do work together in the future."

"You never know," said Mr. Yamamoto.

And after that, she and Gunnar left, at the same time. And began walking down the hall together quickly.

"It will be such a shame not to see you for the next ten years. But I'm booked."

"It was a valiant win," he said. "Your product is brilliant. Anyone can see that."

"Even you. What an incredible, astonishing concession."

"Fair is fair. Best is best. Do you have any plans while you're here in Tokyo?"

"Not really." *Sushi in my hotel room and more of my book.*

"I see. And where are you staying?"

"Down the street."

They got in the elevator together, and the doors

closed. He looked at her, and she looked at him. She smiled. "How are my teeth?"

"Sharp," he said.

"Good. All the better to eat you with and all that."

"And truly, decisively, you have."

"I hope you don't take it too hard."

"All's fair in business."

She grinned. "Indeed."

She doubted that he would think her efforts with her mole on the inside of his corporation for the last few months was fair, but she didn't care. She had killed two birds with one stone. Not only did she have the contract, Gunnar would be out of her life. She could stop obsessing. She could stop waking up drenched in sweat, panting and shaking from a climax she'd had in her sleep because of dream sex with him.

Yeah. She was feeling pretty pleased.

She was hungry for this kind of happiness.

I did it, Dad. I guess you were right, iron did sharpen iron. But it's not him. You sharpened me, and you can be proud of me.

"Where are you staying?"

"I believe we're in the same building," he said.

"Of course we are. It is the nicest hotel within walking distance," she said.

That was one of the many problems with Gunnar. He often employed the same logic she did. There was understanding your enemy, and then there was knowing them just a little bit too well.

They walked into the busy, polished lobby and continued walking across the room together.

"Top floor."

"I'm the same."

They stepped onto another elevator in tandem, and the doors closed. And this time, she could hear her heart beating in her ears.

"Care to have a celebratory drink?" he asked.

"I would," she said.

"Wonderful."

And there was something, something building inside of her. In anticipation, and a feeling. And when the doors opened to the abbreviated hallway that housed the penthouse rooms, he led her down the opposite direction from her own room, his phone granting access to the room immediately.

"After you," he said.

"Thank you."

His penthouse seemed entirely different than hers. This one was all black. A high shine floor, with curved modern art everywhere. All black.

And the large windows that looked out over the city gave a view of the madness below while keeping the occupant at a distance.

"I love Tokyo," she said.

"I prefer the top of the mountain. But as cities go."

She turned, and saw that he was standing in front of the kitchen counter, his hands flat on the glossy dark surface.

Such beautiful hands.

"Yes. But on a mountain you're probably alone."

"I elect to have solitude. I quite like it."

"Not me," she said. "A business meeting. A party, with networking… I love all of it."

Of course, her surrounding life was completely empty. But that was a choice. Because her father had taught her how to network, how to connect in ways that benefitted and suited you, but he'd impressed upon her the importance of guarding herself.

It was like she lived in a constant state of tension with her emotions.

Be friendly, but not known.

It was why she often went so soft after a business event or negotiation.

You could not go as hard as she did in these situations and then not decompress somehow. Usually, a warm bath and a book.

She shouldn't have thought about baths. Not standing there in front of him. Or maybe…

Something changed between them. The quality of the air.

No. She couldn't let her guard down, but she could feel it. Could feel it falling away, and it was too soon.

It was safe to read romance novels alone. Safe to cry alone. Safe to feel alone.

But not in front of him.

They had nothing to discuss. So what was the real reason she was here?

You know why you're here. You came for this.

This was going to be her last interaction with Gunnar Magnusson for a very long time. Maybe they would never compete for the same contract ever again. Their companies were in divergent spaces. And this may have been truly the last and most decisive competition.

This was the moment.

She had been sixteen the first time she thought about kissing him.

It had been a fever dream. Something that had hit her when he had treated her to a derisive smile while he had prepared to go into battle with her father, the first time he had been at the helm of Magnum in a negotiation.

He'd won. And she had spent the flight home feeling guilty, shame filled and confused. Her fantasies had steadily grown more and more adult.

But time, animosity and common sense had not dimmed them.

She'd wanted him six months ago and he'd denied her.

But she wasn't weeping now. She wasn't sad.

She'd just defeated him, so whatever his excuses about her being vulnerable…

He couldn't cling to them now.

And maybe he would still reject her. But she wouldn't have to face him after, so what did it matter?

This was her moment. And she would take it.

"I know my turtlenecks are not to your taste. Maybe I should just…" And without thinking, she grabbed the hem of her shirt and pulled it up over her head.

CHAPTER TWO

OLIVE WATCHED GUNNAR'S expression closely, trying to gauge a response. She had a simple black bra beneath her turtleneck, but honestly, she hadn't planned this, even though now she could see…

There had never been another end point.

Not for her. She had to have this, or try to have it, anyway.

She had given and given to this life, to this dream of her father's—she wanted to give to it. Out of loyalty and love.

But this was something she wanted to take for herself.

Needed to take for herself.

But she couldn't see if it was the same for him. She had no idea what he was thinking. So she stared.

Would he reject her again?

She didn't know what she had expected. For him to laugh. For him to suddenly transform into a charmer of some kind?

Gunnar had quite the reputation as a lover. He was not a playboy, in fact, he did not flaunt his physical relationships at all. But there were whispers. Of his prowess. Of his particular…assets. And of the intensity.

Not that she had looked in online forums for rumors about what it was like to have sex with him.

No. Couldn't be her. At least, she hadn't done it in a while.

He did not smile. He did not put her at ease. But he most certainly didn't laugh. Instead, he reached up and began loosening his tie, stalking toward her, his blue eyes intense, like a predator.

And all the breath in her body whooshed out.

"Oh," she said.

It was the last thing she said before he gathered her up in his arms, and brought his mouth down on to hers in a raging torrent of pent-up passion that threatened to destroy them both.

Finally. Finally. He was kissing her. And it had been worth the wait. Because it was everything. Beyond. It was the pages of every romance novel. The kind where tension and lust burned from the pages and left her weak with wanting. He was a conqueror.

And he plundered her mouth.

It was hot and slick, and even though she hadn't done this before, she had read enough to have an idea. She parted her lips, met each thrust of his tongue with her own. She was ready.

Physically, she might be innocent, but she had a treasure trove of fantasies, and they were not tentative. And they all centered on him.

She wrenched his tie the rest of the way free, pulling it off and throwing it down onto the floor.

"Thank you for being such a gracious loser," she said, wrenching at his shirt, pulling it open and letting buttons fly everywhere.

His chest.

Dear God. That chest.

She ran her hands over it, hungry. Excitement building between her thighs.

Rough golden hair covered tawny skin, the muscles there thick and well defined.

He was everything she had ever fantasized about.

He was more.

He was…

He growled and leaned in, biting her neck. "It was always going to end here, Olive."

Relief swamped her.

He felt it too.

He did.

But the years of learning to guard herself, against him and everything, pushed her to be spiky in return.

"I am not an inevitability," she said.

Except she knew she was. This was. It had been set in stone perhaps since the dawn of time.

Her body was trained to respond only to Gunnar Magnusson, whether it made sense or not. And it didn't. Because he was the antithesis of all that she should want.

Except… She was a smart, ambitious woman, and she could not accept a man who was any less of those things than her. So of course… The modern-day Viking raider who wore a suit with ease, but also looked like he could wield an axe, was all she wanted.

Anything else would be a compromise.

And Olive had never been taught how to compromise.

Conquer. Destroy. Dominate.

The word made her knees feel weak.

Because the truth of it was…

She thrilled at the idea of a man strong enough to dominate her.

A man that she would want to submit to. To let him make her feel the kinds of pleasure he dictated.

And that, well that, was exactly why Gunnar appealed to her, even while driving her crazy.

"For me you are."

And that was when he pushed his hand down beneath the waistband of her pants, her panties, his big, rough fingers sliding between that damp cleft there, finding her wet and ready. "Is this not inevitable, Olive?"

And it was the strain in his voice that nearly sent her over the edge.

The way the ferocity in his gaze stood as an admission to his own desire.

That she wasn't simply claiming this for herself, but that he was claiming it for him too.

Which made it theirs.

Oh, this fire was theirs and that drove her higher, faster.

He stroked her, rubbing her sensitized flesh with the pad of his finger, before thrusting it deep inside of her.

She gasped, grabbing hold of his broad shoulders. "Gunnar."

"It feels inevitable to me. You're so wet for me. This cannot be the first time you've ever thought of giving yourself to me. You must think about it. Often. Not just that night you tried to kiss me."

And she wanted to admit it. That he was the only man she'd ever wanted. That she'd dreamed of him for years. That when she'd turned eighteen she had a fevered fantasy of sneaking to see him—another birthday that she had in office buildings, because of her father's business dealings. Another time when Gunnar had been in a hotel room close to hers.

And she had thought… She was legally an adult, and could go to his bed if she wanted to.

In the end, she had been too afraid to do it.

She'd been too afraid of his rejection.

And she would have him now, in honor of eighteen-year-old Olive. She would not tell him that she had fantasized about him. She would not tell him how long she'd wanted him.

And she would not allow him to believe that they were inevitable.

She'd been taught to guard her feelings all of her life, and she could see the benefit to that now.

She felt shaken and vulnerable already. Guarding the deepest part of herself was necessary.

He could believe in the attraction. The physical aspect of it. But she couldn't expose her sweet, girlish fantasies of him. Couldn't let him know about that soft, secret part of herself.

Except then he pushed a second finger inside of her,

his blue eyes boring into hers as he thrust them in and out of her willing body.

"You are enjoying this," he growled.

She moved her hand to cup the front of his pants. "So are you."

It was an effort, not to react to what she found there. Hard and so large that the virginal nerves she didn't think she possessed rose up hard.

He moved his hand away from her, and she felt bereft when he left her body. But then, he reached around and undid her bra, and there was something about finally being exposed to him like this that only amped up her arousal.

She pushed his jacket from his shoulders, then his shirt. Then she moved away from him, kicking off her shoes, and pushing her pants and underwear down her hips, relieved. That finally she was naked in front of him.

Finally.

She sat on the black, velvet couch in the living area, in that perfect, ladylike manner she had been instructed to sit in charm school. And it amused her. To act prim even now.

His lips curved into a smile, his hands going to his belt. And every part of her went liquid at the sight. He undid it slowly, moving the belt through his palms, and snapping it, the sound sending a jolt of anticipation and desire through her body.

"You are something, aren't you?" he asked.

"How long have *you* fantasized about me?" she asked, because he was happy to try and force her to admit that this was a long-held desire, so why shouldn't she push for the same?

"Probably not a good question to ask."

He began to undo the closure on his pants. Kicked off his shoes and socks, and stripped off everything else.

His erection was thick and long, and while she had been absolutely certain that nothing about the man would be diminutive—plus there had been those online rumors—she wasn't certain she had been prepared for him to be quite so… Much.

"Spread your legs," he said.

She met his gaze, because she was never one to back away from a challenge, most especially a challenge issued by Gunnar.

She sat poised on the edge of the couch, and opened herself for him. He stood there, devouring her with his eyes, and even though he was not touching her… She felt that blue lightning as if he were stroking her.

She moved her hand, ready to ease the ache herself.

"No," he said, and that stopped her midmotion.

"You will not come until I say you can."

"That's quite misogynistic," she said.

"I think some people call it a game, Olive. If you play games with me, you follow rules. Do you understand?"

She was shivering now. Uncontrollably. Because this really was her every fantasy. Every dark, shameful need brought to the surface, bright and sharp.

He walked toward her, every inch the conqueror, and

reached out and took hold of her chin. Then he leaned down, and he kissed her.

It was hot, deep and dirty. A pantomime of what he would do to other parts of her body, that hot tongue thrusting deep, creating havoc in her core.

Still poised on the edge of the couch, he kept her head tilted up as he stood, and then he moved forward, fisting his large erection, and guiding it toward her lips.

She parted them eagerly. Greedily, and took the shiny head of him inside. And then he canted his hips forward, pushing himself deeper into her mouth.

She sucked him greedily, wrapping her fingers around the base of his shaft and squeezing tight as she took in as much of him as she could.

This was her fantasy. From the submissive position, making this man weak with desire.

She had thought of it so many times. And while it felt new, while it felt like a first time, it also felt as if she had some idea of what to do.

She had read about the act, described explicitly, and her own mind had run wild with scenarios where she might end up in a position to do this to him. In a limousine. Shared on the way to a conference, for some reason. Beneath the boardroom table. After a tense negotiation. Yes. Her mind had well and truly been over this territory before. She was lost in it. In the rhythm. In the dark magic of it all.

And then suddenly he drew away from her. "Enough. It's my turn."

And he knelt down, lifting her up by the waist and sitting her atop the arm of the couch. He guided her to use her arm to brace herself on the back of it, and to use the other hand to grip the edge. Then he roughly parted her legs, one propped up on the couch, the other on the floor. And he wrapped his hands around, cupping her ass as he leaned forward and began to eat her.

It was not tentative. He devoured her like a beast, sucking her clitoris into his mouth, before pushing two fingers inside of her to create a hypnotic rhythm, lips and tongue working in tandem with his magic hands.

She writhed against his mouth, his beard rough on her inner thighs. His tongue hot and obscene.

"Gunnar," she moaned, fisting his hair and rocking her hips in time with his thrusts.

"You can come now," he said, sliding the flat of his tongue over that sensitized bundle of nerves, and making her world shatter behind her eyelids.

She couldn't stop. Wave after wave of desire crashing over her. And when she was done, holding that same position, he shifted and pressed his arousal between her legs, teasing her as he rubbed the glossy head over where she needed him most.

"Please," she whimpered. "Please."

"What?"

"Take me, you monster," she said, the words coming out random.

"Oh. That's what you want from me, little Olive? You want me to take you and make this all go away?"

"Yes," she moaned.

And then, he was right there, sinking into her, filling her. It was tight, but it was glorious.

And she let her head fall back. Her keening cry so

loud it should've embarrassed her. But she couldn't be embarrassed. All she could do was feel.

"It will never go away," he whispered against her mouth. "You will want me. Always. You will never be free of this." He began to rock his hips forward, going deeper, deeper still. And his thrusts became hard, erratic, and she thought she was going to die from the wave of pleasure that threatened to capsize her.

Then he lifted her up off the couch, still buried deep inside of her, and walked them both out of the room. He separated from her a moment, to lay her down on the bed, where she knew she was open and glistening and obvious to him, and she didn't even care.

Then he was on her, over her, thrusting hard back inside of her and making them both cry out with the glory of it.

"You'll think about me," she whispered. "You'll think about me forever. I promise you."

"Then give me everything now," he said.

And she found herself breaking apart again, shivering and shaking, this climax deeper, different than the first. And then, he snapped. He growled, fierce and like the Viking raider she knew he was in his soul, as he spilled himself deep inside of her.

It was done.

She had done it. It should be a thick, permanent line drawn beneath them.

Why then, did she shiver? Why was she trembling from the inside out? Why did she feel like weeping?

Why did she feel lost?

"Congratulations," he said. And then he got up off

the bed and went into the bathroom. She lay there for a long moment, and then stood slowly, making her way back into the living room and collecting her clothes.

She felt rocked. Scraped raw, but she forced a smile on her face.

She had won. In every way she had won.

She had the contract. She wouldn't have to see Gunnar again.

She would not indulge this pain in her chest telling her she had lost something.

And before she had cut ties, she had finally lived her deepest fantasy. And it had been everything… Everything. And now when she went to bed alone… She would have the real thing to think about. And not just wild fantasies based on fiction.

And of course, she had always known that she and Gunnar could never have more than one night. It was impossible.

But this night had been everything she needed it to be.

She didn't need any more.

CHAPTER THREE

WHEN HE SAW Olive Monroe's name come across his desk two months later, he was almost certain that it was a hallucination.

She had been haunting him, like a ghost, so it seemed in keeping with everything else. He woke up at night, tangled in his sheets, slick with sweat.

Gunnar did not do unsatisfied desire.

When he wanted something, he got it. Whether it was a chocolate cupcake or a woman. But thus was the longstanding issue of Olive Monroe.

There was no other person on the planet he understood quite so well.

And none who was buried so deeply beneath his skin.

Were he another sort of man, he might have called it…love.

But he was not that man, so he called it fascination, or even just protective.

From the time she'd been a beautiful eighteen-year-old girl, looking at him with hungry eyes and uncertain desire.

Because yes, he took what he wanted, but within the bonds of moral certainty. Women who knew what they wanted, and who wanted him. And who well knew the desires and needs of their own bodies.

He'd known what her desire was for. What it meant. He could have shown her then, but he'd…

He'd made his life a pursuit of being nothing like Magnus Ragnarson.

His father had been a bastard of the highest order, and the only thing worse than the man's actions, had been the years Gunnar had spent idolizing him. Not realizing the manner of man he truly was.

It was his desire to be nothing like the kind of man who used and discarded young women, who engaged in morally bankrupt business practices that destroyed the environment, displaced families and paid workers piteous wages to work in dangerous factories, that had held him back from ever touching Olive.

And yet it had done nothing to dampen his desire for her.

His obsession.

He did not spar with her because he needed to indulge the public spectacle. He had no use for such things. He sparred with her because he enjoyed it.

He sparred with her because it was better than sex with anyone else.

Turning her away the night of her father's funeral had been a feat of unhuman strength. Certainly, it had fueled a sense of moral superiority in him that had nearly been consolation enough for not tasting her sweet mouth.

He'd given in now, though.

And he'd considered calling her many times over the last two months. Why should they not have an affair?

Self-denial had so long been his virtue when it came to her that he'd resisted it out of habit.

But his body wanted a particular woman. And that was another thing about Gunnar. He did not take second. When he wanted something, he would have the *first* of it. The best of it. Or he would have none of it.

And so his lust had remained thoroughly unsated these past two months, because all his body wanted was Olive.

But no. It was not a hallucination. Olive's name truly was on this memo, and his assistant was standing there fidgeting, the man looking utterly ill at ease.

"All of the information is here in this written memo," he said. "But I feel also that I need to speak to you."

"Make it quick."

"Do you know how Olive was able to win the auto contract?"

It was no mystery to Gunnar. The simple truth was… Olive had destroyed his presentation. Hers had been better in every way. Her product was better. He had been…fiercely proud of her.

"I am always happy to receive a bit of insight," he said.

"She had seen your products. And your presentation."

Something in him went still. "That is impossible."

"It isn't," the man said. "Because… Because she paid me. To feed her the information."

It was as if the world had been turned on its axis. Gunnar was immobilized. He prided himself on his read of people. For being wrong about someone had destroyed his world, and the lives of the people he had loved most, and he had learned that he could not afford to make such mistakes again, not ever.

And here he was now, faced with the betrayal of his assistant, and…

Olive.

Olive, who he'd long wanted to protect. To save.

Olive who he…

In his mind was a montage of every time he'd brought her a cupcake. Every time they'd sparred. Of the time he'd lifted her from a potted plant when she'd been an ungainly teenage girl—long before he'd wanted her.

Of the first moment he'd realized he did want her. And of the strange mix of pride and competition he'd always felt when watching her work.

He'd always found her brilliant. A much brighter mind than her father. And he'd believed her to be… good.

But she was no different than all these men who played games to line their pockets. Than those who disadvantaged others to elevate themselves.

Little Olive, who he had always believed to be singular, was nothing more than a common thief.

Everything in him turned to ice. "So, you've been working for her?"

"Yes," Jason said.

"I would venture to say you are not coming clean

now because of a guilty conscience." Clearly neither Jason nor Olive had a conscience at all.

"No," the other man said, hesitating.

"Then why?" Gunnar pressed.

"Because I don't feel her company is the future. There are issues… There are issues at the moment. Vulnerabilities."

"In what sense," Gunnar asked, his voice hard.

"She hasn't been herself. Everyone on her team has noticed. She has been at work less, coming in late. One wonders if she's slid into the sorts of traps that many people her age might in this position."

"What are you saying?"

"Maybe a drinking problem? Partying? I'm not certain. All I know is it's becoming clear she may not be the future of the company I initially believed."

Even now, he wanted to defend Olive. She was young and saddled with an incredible burden.

She isn't who you thought.

He cast his mind back to the night of her father's funeral. How she'd wept. How soft she'd been.

That had been a lie like everything else. Because how could that woman who had betrayed him also be that soft creature who'd tilted her face up to him in silent demand for a kiss?

"What is it you want?" Gunnar asked.

"I want a position secured at the company. I can provide proof she earned the contract nefariously, and you can get her out of the way and secure a contract with Yamamoto yourself."

Gunnar laughed. And laughed.

"I do not negotiate with traitors who have no honor. Clean out your desk."

Olive was wretched. She had been feeling sick for weeks, and she was in utter denial about why. She simply couldn't handle the potential truth. And she had avoided thinking about it. Completely. It made her feel like she was shaking apart.

She didn't think it was a mystery as to why she hadn't had her period two months in a row. It wasn't a mystery why she was feeling groggy and tired and sick in the mornings. Not when you considered she had sex for the first time in her life, and it had been *decidedly* unprotected.

She and Gunnar were two of the greatest minds in technology, and they were also two idiots who'd had sex without a condom.

She blamed him. Really.

She had been a virgin. He ought to know better. And all right, maybe she ought to know better too. But she made a terrible choice. They had made a terrible choice. And now, the consequences were…

Well, the consequences were particularly and potentially dire.

She'd…ruined everything. She was supposed to be the guiding light for this company and she was barely able to sit up straight at her desk. She wasn't a pillar of leadership. She'd been fuzzy and disorganized for weeks, her brain a total mess.

She'd gotten herself pregnant with the enemy's baby. Her father would be…

He wouldn't be proud. Not of this.

She was slumped behind her desk, but nobody was here. So it didn't matter.

She took a sleeve of saltines from the top drawer and brought it down, holding it close to her chest. This was really just awful.

She was feeling wretched. And terrified. She had come out on top when it came to the contract, but when it came to everything else…

She had not gotten him out of her system, not if what she suspected was true. If what she suspected was true was, in fact, true then… He was quite a bit more in her system than she had anticipated him ever being.

The idea made her want to throw up then and there.

And suddenly, she heard a commotion outside, a scuffling and then commotion.

And suddenly, the door to her office swung open.

She popped her head up like a meerkat coming up from underground, and then she saw him, and shrank down slightly, so that she was certain only her eyes were visible over the top of her desk.

"Olive," he said, her name on his lips a warning.

"What's going on, bestie?" she asked, trying her best to paste a bright and convincing smile on her face.

She had a feeling it looked more like a grimace.

He rounded the desk, and she scrabbled downward, pulling her knees up to her chest, the sleeve of saltines held tightly against them.

"Did you think that you could get away with this?"

Terror streaked through her. How could he know? She didn't even *know*.

"I don't know what you're talking about," she whispered.

"Your unfortunate foray into corporate espionage."

She was almost relieved to hear him say that. And how ridiculous was that? Except the company didn't seem like the important thing, not right now. Not between them.

So she tried her best to look and sound casual, even while she was shaking apart.

"Oh. That. All's fair," she said, brushing some crumbs off of her knee. And suddenly, his blue eyes sharpened.

"What exactly are you doing?"

"I am having a sick day," she said.

"You're in the office," he pointed out.

She shrugged her shoulders and took a saltine out of the cracker tube, because really, there was no pretending this wasn't happening. He had caught her in an inglorious position and she refused to scramble out of it, which in her mind would be giving in. Bending to the pressure of his presence, and she refused to do that.

"If there's work to be done, I'm here. Just with crackers."

"You are on the floor."

"Yeah. They did a study? In Sweden. It was very obscure. You probably haven't heard of it. But it was about the increase of workflow when you sit in unconventional spaces. Something about the freedom to shape your body how you feel you ought to."

"Olive," he said, harder this time.

And just then, the absurdity of all of it crashed over her. He was her mortal enemy in many ways, always had been. Trained up from the time they were children, essentially. And in other ways, he was the person she knew best left in all this world. Her father was gone, and aching grief that hadn't eased up even once in the last six months, and she had never had time to have friends. As far as she knew, Gunnar didn't have friends either.

He had lovers.

Which she supposed she was now among. But they actually did know each other. And right now, she wanted to confide her woes in him, except he was the source of them, and he could never know.

He made her feel guilty for having double-crossed him, and that was ridiculous.

His father had certainly taught him the same values as hers. When it came to business, nothing was off the table, her dad had been clear on that. And that Magnus had acted in the same fashion.

"Well. If all is fair, then you will appreciate what comes next," he said.

He crouched down in front of her, and she felt her stomach get tight.

He grabbed the edge of the cracker packet, and tugged it out of her hands. "I shall need you paying attention. And not eating crackers."

"I didn't eat crackers in bed," she said. "You can't be too annoyed by the crackers."

"You did not eat crackers in bed, you did not stay long enough to have a snack."

"I wasn't aware snacks were on the table, so to speak."

His eyes flashed with ice. "They weren't."

"See. There was no point bringing it up, then," she said weakly.

"You were the one that mentioned bed."

"So I did."

And he just sort of looked at her, those blue eyes piercing deeper than she would like.

"I'm going to ruin you."

He said it conversationally. As he had said everything else since he had walked in.

"What?"

"You know, what you did is illegal. In many jurisdictions."

"Well, you're going to have trouble figuring out which jurisdiction exactly I did it in. We both travel all over the world, we have corporate offices all over the world." She was terrified, her heart beating so hard she felt dizzy.

And worse, she felt guilty.

Because Gunnar was angry, and that she had expected. But there was a sense she'd…disappointed him.

And she hated it.

But she couldn't do anything but brazen it out now. Her dad hadn't taught her how to back down. He'd only taught her to dig in.

And right now, defending herself had never been more important.

Because it was quite possible she contained a life.

"I know that at least at one point you were somewhere where it was illegal. As it was Jason committing the espionage, and he is my assistant."

"That little weasel. He ratted me out didn't he?"

"Can a weasel rat something? Or is it… A weaseling?"

"I don't know, and I don't care," she returned, ferociously. She leaned forward and snatched her crackers out of his hand, and stood up. But all at once, the blood left her head, and she felt woozy.

"Gunnar?" It was the last thing she said, and his face was the last thing she saw, before she collapsed into his arms.

CHAPTER FOUR

GUNNAR HAD NEVER taken Olive for being weak. She had always seemed strong and plucky and well able to dish out and take the same.

But here she was, collapsed into his arms, fainted dead away, and he knew that it wasn't a ruse. Because there was no way that she could contrive to have her lips turn that worryingly bluish tint.

And there was no question that he must take action.

Gunnar lifted her up, carrying her out of the front of the office.

And everybody outside looked up at him as if he had murdered her.

"She fainted," he said, growled. "Does anyone have water?"

"I…" The woman behind the counter looked nervous.

And no one was jumping to attention. No one was making movements—frantic or otherwise—to see to the health of their clearly unwell boss.

A drinking problem, Jason had said, but this was not alcohol.

She was ill.

"Ridiculous," he said, striding down the hall, holding Olive to his chest. He was furious with her. For not being what he'd believed her to be.

That realization caught hard in his chest.

He had been on the verge of strangling her, and then, he had found her crouched in a corner eating crackers.

Something wasn't right about this, and he knew that.

But then, something wasn't right about any of this. It was that damned woman. The way that she had gotten him to let his guard down. He had to wonder if she had been running a long con all this time. Had gotten him to see her as someone formidable, but ultimately fluffy. Someone he wanted to protect as much as he wanted to spar with her.

He had brought her cupcakes, and it had started as a joke, and then he had been amused by the fact that she expected them.

But he wondered if somewhere in there, he had allowed her to get between a crack in the wall.

He had begun to feel for her. Deeply.

And now…

She had betrayed him. And it burned.

He had set about to live a life that needed no one. That was not dependent on others to be good or true or right, because he knew he could not trust them to be.

But somewhere along the way he'd grown complacent about her, and too confident in his own ability to discern who was right and good.

He had let her get beneath his defenses.

Never again.

Even now, while he felt obligated to see to her health, he hardened himself against her. Against those feelings.

An interesting question to ask himself as he carried her limp form through the lobby of her high-rise office building, and out the revolving doors. His driver pulled up to the curb. "Take me to the nearest private doctor. I will pay whatever expense, but I don't know what is the matter with her."

"Did you poison her?" the driver asked.

Everyone knew about his rivalry with Olive. It was legendary. A thing written about in the press. Their competition for contracts was a highly sought out show.

And sometimes he thought that people reviewed both of their work simply to see them in action.

He had thought—many times—about farming that part of the business out, but...

You like sparring with her. You like being with her.

It was so raw, so much an apparent weakness now, that it shamed him.

Now he needed to get her to a doctor. What he liked or didn't like about sparring with her was immaterial.

He carried her limp form up to the edge of the sidewalk, and jerked open the passenger door, sitting her inside and scooting her across the seat. Then he got in beside her. He shut the door behind him, and for the first time, she stirred.

His driver took off, melting into the New York traffic.

"What?"

"Oh," she said. "I feel sick."

"If you throw up in my car, there will be a steep cleaning deposit."

"What about if I throw up in your lap?" she asked.

"I don't know. No one has ever done it. I would imagine the consequences would be interesting."

"Oh," she said. "I feel like I'm going to die."

And this made his heart twist, because no matter his anger, whenever he saw a bit of vulnerability in Olive it called to the Viking warrior within him, who wanted to shield her from all danger.

Including himself.

"Are you?" he asked.

"Am I what?"

"Going to die."

"That depends on if you're going to kill me," she said.

"I said *ruin*. Not kill."

She was half lying in the seat, her hand pressed against her forehead. And suddenly, it was as if she had taken in her surroundings for the first time.

"Where are we going?"

"I'm taking you to a doctor, you silly woman. You are clearly unwell."

"No," she said, suddenly scrambling into a sitting position. "I don't need to go to a doctor. Dump me in the gutter with the rest of the traitorous gutter weasels. You want revenge, right? Leave me out in the cold!"

"You collapsed into my arms in your office. I found you on the floor eating a sleeve of crackers. You may be dehydrated. It's likely that you need an infusion of liquid."

"I think I fainted because of my shock at seeing you. And your threats. If you take me to a doctor, I might well just have you arrested for assault."

He lifted one brow. "Will you?"

"A doctor can prove that I was under duress because of you and your words."

"Somehow, I do not think that the doctor will find that I am the cause of your duress."

She laughed. And laughed and laughed. And he had no idea why. "That's just… That's just a hoot. Really. High art. Great comedy."

"I do not understand you."

"No. That's fine." She seemed to curl up into a ball then, as he had found her at the desk.

"Olive," he said, his tone terse now. "What is going on?"

"You're the one that knows everything. Why don't you tell me? Why don't you tell me everything? Including how you plan to ruin me."

"Oh. It is very simple. I want Ambient to become a subsidiary of Magnum."

Because one thing was clear, even as part of him wanted to protect her. There was only one true punishment for this transgression.

"You want to buy me out?"

"Yes."

"I feel like that violates multiple antitrust laws, Gunnar. And there's no way that you're going to be allowed to do that."

"I disagree. There are other major tech corporations."

"Any as big as ours?"

"As big as yours. And anyway, my company has other facets to it."

"Why would I agree to that?"

"Because the alternative is prison. You will find."

"Really. You would really have me arrested?"

"Think about it. Do you think that your father would really have had my father arrested?"

"Well. You know he would have."

"And do you think that I should spare you because you are a woman? Is that how this is going to go?"

"Yes," she said. "I'm a girl. You can't send a girl to prison."

"Last I checked, they had prisons for girls."

Olive huffed, the sound practically a hiss. "That is incredibly unkind."

He could see she did not truly believe he would do it.

"Was it unkind of you to go about snooping into my affairs when you should not? And then... Seducing me?"

"Seducing you," she said. "Ha! Seducing you. Last I checked, I wasn't the one with the entire online forums dedicated to my sexual prowess, Gunnar. So I would assume, that if anyone had done the seducing..."

"Was I the one that took my shirt off in the middle of my living room?"

"Well. No. But. Some people would consider a steady stream of chocolate cupcakes to be foreplay."

"I'm not going to deny it."

"What I wanted," she said, leaning in, "was to have it all done. All of it. I didn't want to see you anymore. I wanted to come out on top in business, and I wanted to deal with this… This thing. It's always been there. You know it. I know it. We ignore it. We go into boardrooms and we spar, and by the time I'm done I feel like I need a cigarette and I've never even had a cigarette. It's the most… The most invigorating, infuriating thing, and I needed something to… To finish it. Because you know, Gunnar, when fighting with the man I hate most in the world excites me more than making out with a different man, something is wrong. I just wanted to… I just wanted to be done with it. That's all."

There was something about the admission that humanized her again. That tempted him to look at her and see his Olive. The one he had cared for all this time.

But she had revealed herself to be untrustworthy.

And even if not…

He might have cared, but he'd never touched her all those years and it had been for a reason.

He'd felt deep affection for her but he'd never planned on having her in his life. He didn't do romance. He didn't do love in that sense.

It was one thing to feel protective toward her from a distance, to care for her well-being, her safety. But he'd never wanted a wife or children, and he'd never thought to drag a woman into his life in that way.

So he'd never touched her, because he'd known he would only hurt her.

And she hurt you instead.

No. He was not hurt.

He was furious.

"It was a lovely speech," he said. "Are you finished?"

"I'm finished."

"We will continue speaking about this when the doctor has had his say."

She looked out the window. "Where are we?"

"The doctor."

She gave him a narrow-eyed look.

It was a plush facility. Private, and they were ushered in immediately, where Olive's vitals were taken, and her temperature checked, while she was cocooned in a blanket on a velvet couch.

"I don't need a doctor," she protested.

"You seem to be dehydrated," the intake nurse said.

Gunnar lifted a shoulder. "What did I tell you?"

"And what is this? You just can't send me to prison until you make sure I'm properly hydrated? That's very strange."

"I like my opponents to be healthy. For the same reason I don't engage in corporate espionage, Olive. I like my playing fields even. All the better to prove that I am the best. I can see how you failed on that score."

"If you proceed through the door," the nurse said. "You will find a restroom. We'll take a urine sample, and then we'll work on getting you some liquid."

"I don't want to give a urine sample," she said.

"Oh," the woman said.

And Gunnar thought… Well, he thought that he had not imagined he would be sitting in this place, listening to Olive discuss what sorts of samples she was willing to give the doctor, but it was strange to him that she did not wish to give this one.

"We are very discreet," the nurse said. "If narcotics are detected…"

"It's not… I don't do drugs," Olive said. "It's nothing like that. It's just… Invasion of privacy. And I don't want to do it. I have a phobia of lab cups. They scare me."

"Why exactly?"

And he walked his mind backward. Through all of this. Through coming into her office and finding her eating saltines. To her passing out. To her combative behavior.

And now the fact that she did not wish to give this sample. And if it was not drugs, as she was quick to state—and he believed it, because for all that Olive was a competitive and strange creature, he could not see her taking a risk with her brain, and substances— well, he could think then of only one thing.

"Olive," he said, his voice a growl. "Are you pregnant?"

CHAPTER FIVE

OLIVE FELT AS if the rich brocade walls in this very strange doctor's office had come crashing down around her. She made her eyes as round as possible. "Not that I'm aware of."

"Do you suspect?" he pressed, his voice a growl.

"I don't… I don't…"

"Go in and take the test," he said.

She did all she could to make herself sink more heavily into her seat. "You can't make me."

"Olive," he said.

"I…"

Her face drained of all color. "Do not pass out," he commanded.

"You can't tell someone not to pass out," she said. "You're unreasonable. Barking orders like that. A person doesn't choose to pass out, it just happens. And if you keep looking at me like that, all the blood is going to drain out of my head and I am actually going to do it. I'm going to faint dead away at your feet. And you just said you didn't want that, so maybe you should try being less of a scary jackass."

She was breathing hard, her hand pressed to her forehead again. "I don't… I don't… It's just that… It could be many other things."

"It likely couldn't be," the nurse said.

"There are a lot of reasons that women miss their periods."

"Mostly it's pregnancy," the nurse said.

Olive felt dizzy. She'd trained her whole life to run her father's company. She knew how to focus on that at the exclusion of everything else.

She didn't know how to be a mother.

She'd never even considered the possibility.

Facing the prospect of her whole world changing like this….

She couldn't bear it.

"It was just two periods."

"Likely pregnancy," the woman said.

"I did not ask," Olive said, directing her ire at the poor woman sitting there looking white-faced and unsure of what to do. Olive had a feeling that she was about the same color. The pallor of being confronted with her potential pregnancy—a word she had not even wanted to think—with Gunnar in the room was… Far too much.

"Though I bet if I was you wouldn't send me to prison," she said, laughing weekly. It really was a terrible joke. Then, all of it was.

"Go and take the test. Prioritize the results," he said to the nurse.

And Olive found herself obeying. All the while, she thought she would find a way to slip out the back. But there was no back. The bathroom was as beautiful and lush as the rest of the place, with pink wallpaper and a crushed velvet chaise lounge in the corner. "Great. A fainting couch. I needed one earlier."

The little lab cups seemed utterly at odds with the rest of the place. Clinical, where the rest of it wasn't. And it did not take long for her to gather a sample, and leave it in the little two-sided cabinet in the wall.

She sat down on the couch for a second, and then laid on it.

Her heart was pounding. What would she do? What would they do?

Right now, she had no idea what he would do, and that was the terrifying question in all of this.

Gunnar was furious with her. Absolutely mad with outrage. And he had every right to be, she supposed. She had found all these ways to try and justify her actions. Things that had made it all seem… Reasonable. Yes. She had found ways to make it feel reasonable. But it wasn't. And she knew that.

She had just been so… So desperate. Desperate to get away from him. Desperate to do something about the feelings that rioted through her body whenever she saw him. Desperate to please her father and set herself up as the CEO he'd trained her to be.

It had been the culmination of everything. Putting her one weakness behind her, claiming her future, her fated future.

And now it was all in doubt.

There was a soft knock on the door.

"I'm just resting," she snapped.

"It's only me," said the nurse, opening the door. And she came in, her eyes looking soft.

"Did you already talk to him about the results?"

The nurse shook her head. "No. They're your results, Olive, not his. I don't know the nature of your relationship with him…"

"Really? Do you not watch the news?"

"All right," the nurse said, holding up a conciliatory hand. "I am attempting to not know who either of you are. Because that is part of my job at a place like this. I don't make any assumptions, and I certainly don't make any judgments."

"Go ahead," said Olive. "Judge away. I judge myself."

"Too bad about privacy laws. Because there is a very large office pool that concerns whether or not the two of you are actually secretly sleeping together. And I could clearly win."

"Really?"

The woman looked at her gravely. "They worship you."

"Do they?" Olive asked. "How weird. I would've thought that… Anyway. Never mind. What are the results?"

"You already know, sweetheart," the woman said.

And immediately, tears began to slide down her cheeks, and she was so grateful that the woman had brought these results to her in confidence, because Olive didn't think she could have stomached crying like this in front of Gunnar.

And who else did she have?

What a strange, dysfunctional, lonely existence she had. Her father was gone, she'd never known her mother, and now she wanted them both so badly.

Except…

Her father would be so disappointed in her. That feeling was like a crushing weight now. He wouldn't have been happy to be a grandfather. He would question her suitability. Ask how she'd been so weak, so foolish as to get herself pregnant with the enemy's baby.

He would ask how he'd managed to fail her so badly that she had exercised no control at all.

"I don't know what I'm going to do."

"Well. The rest is up to you. He doesn't get to have the results. You can tell him whatever you want."

But she knew there was no lying to Gunnar Magnusson. He saw everything with those sharp blue eyes, and Olive well knew it.

But she needed to get herself together. She could not go out there looking like this. She could not go out there with tears running down her face. She refused to let him see her weak.

And that's all he'd seen, all day. She'd been doing her best to brazen it out, to smile through it, to banter and make jokes, but she would not show weakness now.

"Okay. I just need a minute."

She took a breath, and she steeled herself. She reminded herself of why she had made all the choices she'd made in the last few months. They'd made sense.

And she would find sense at the end of this too. But she was not a coward, and she wouldn't hide.

She was Olive Monroe, CEO of Ambient technologies, and she had been trained to handle every single thing that was thrown at her. And Gunnar was…well, he was Gunnar. But as genetics went…

Hell, this baby was going to be a genius.

This baby… As it was a foregone conclusion that she would be having the baby.

A little voice inside of her nudged her. *You know that it is.*

Of course, she would need the baby to work for her, and not for Gunnar.

Will then. That had allowed her to put something into a category. And that felt… Reassuring. In a very strange way.

She took a deep, fortifying breath, and went back out to the room that Gunnar was in. But then, the nurse met her again. "IV," she said.

And she found herself ushered into a gloriously beautiful bedroom, where she was stuck like she was a little pincushion, and wrapped up in blankets again, as they began to feed liquid directly into her veins.

What an indignity.

And Gunnar was there for all of it, standing there looking forbidding, his arms crossed across his broad chest.

"Well," she said, attempting to find some sort of haughty manner, even if she was wrapped in an extremely fluffy blanket, her arm propped up on a stack of pillows, and her face poking out as if it was a sea of blankets and she was barely keeping her head above the surface. "I'm pregnant," she said. "So. Interesting."

"Interesting is not the word I would use," he said. His voice hard.

"Oh. Well, don't worry about it. You might not be the father."

His gaze did something terrifying then. And she was transported back to the medieval Viking books that she enjoyed reading.

He looked every inch the marauder. Ready to do something… Drastic.

"Is that so?" he asked, his voice deceptively quiet.

"I mean, it's been… Two months? It's… You never know. Things happen…"

"Do I have the right to assume then, that you have taken a string of other lovers since coming to my bed?"

"Well, you make it sound as if you're not just part of the string of lovers. The ones that came before, the ones that came after. You're acting as if you were a singular event, Gunnar."

"And you are on dangerous ground, Olive Monroe. Is this my baby?"

"I don't have a crystal ball," she said, feeling sick.

Of course it was his baby. She had never even seen another naked man, much less had sex with one. She had never wanted anyone but him. This was… This was so twisted. Such a strange expression of a girl-hood fantasy gone wrong.

But she wanted to wrench back some of the control here. She didn't want to be the only one that was con-fused and out of sorts. She didn't want to be the one without…any power.

Her father had taught her to never go into a business deal without leverage. She needed time to find leverage.

Or even a foothold.

She was in shock.

As if it wasn't a completely logical thing that if you had unprotected sex you might find yourself pregnant.

But the first time? It just seemed… Like a bad lottery. People tried really hard to get pregnant.

She had just been trying to feel something. To feel him.

To finally give in to the experience that his eyes, his hands and his body had been promising her for all of these years, and now here she was.

CHAPTER SIX

IT WOULD'VE BEEN nearly amusing, the howl of rage that Olive let out, if he were not half so angry himself. This woman, this woman who had tied him in knots for years—when he allowed nothing to touch him, nothing to reach him—was now carrying his child.

Or not, she said.

As if there was a doubt.

And he'd have said she wasn't. That he was sure she could not be, but it turned out he didn't know her at all, and also that when it came to Olive he could not trust himself.

Few things would have outraged him half so much as that fact alone.

Add in that she was pregnant, and his rage was an Icelandic volcano.

"Your heir," she said. "Your heir. I am the owner of one of the biggest tech companies in the entire world—"

"Soon to be former owner, though, I will keep you as CEO. Your image is a very important one. It's part of the brand. I would never mess with such good branding."

She did not seem quite so concerned about being tethered to an IV when she scrambled out of the nest of blanket she was in. "I will not lose my company to you."

"Are you only just now taking me seriously?" He could see by the look in her eyes, that she was. That she hadn't truly believed he was serious before. "If you play with dragons, you must expect to be burned, Olive. Your protestations are weak. You should've thought of it before you dared cross me. This is not a game. And it never was. Chocolate cupcakes notwithstanding. People enjoyed the show of you and I, and I find you amusing. But much like a child who needs to be taken in hand, clearly, you did not understand the severity of the consequences that lay before you. I am not to be trifled with."

"Neither am I," she said, rage seeping from her every pore.

And even now, even now with her looking wretched, dressed in that black turtleneck and black pants—the only thing she ever wore, and he would change that if she were his—her brown hair tied back in a low bun, and no makeup on her face, she was delectable.

Because he could well remember exactly how she had tasted. Exactly how it had felt to slide into her tight, wet heat. She had been so tight. So glorious.

And the fact that she had other lovers since then should enrage him—he had not been able to even look at another woman since he'd been with her—but instead, he found himself hard and throbbing as ever.

What she did to him was unacceptable.

It always had been, but before he had... He had wanted to protect her. From himself, and from the world. He'd felt...in awe of her. Proud of her. He'd used that pride to explain his attraction. The ferocity of it.

Now he had to face the fact he was but a basic man who had been blinded by the needs of his body.

She was not special. She was merely good at deceit.

She was not singular.

He would not forget that again.

And he sat there, watching as the bag drained. Watching as some color returned to her face.

They did not speak. And when the cycle was through, the nurse came in and detached her from the bag, taking the needle from her arm.

"Do you need some assistance getting her out to the car?" the nurse said.

"Oh, no need."

And he swept her up out of the bed, taking the blankets with her. "I will make sure she's comfortable."

He expected her to fight, but instead, she was suspiciously limp, and he found he did not enjoy it. He preferred her hissing. He preferred her fighting.

But she seemed suddenly exhausted.

He carried her back to the street, to his car.

"To the airport," he said.

"I don't even have anything with me," she said. "Someone needs to feed my goldfish."

"You have a goldfish?"

She seemed reinvigorated all of a sudden, and he was glad of that.

"No," she said. "But I *could*."

"You couldn't, and we both know it. And if you did, there would be some method of feeding it by way of telephone app, I assume."

"Telephone app. For all that you're a tech wizard sometimes you sound a hundred years old."

"An issue with my understanding of the language, perhaps."

"I don't think that's true."

It wasn't. He had spoken English from the time he was a boy. In fact, really, his only investment in hanging onto his accent was that he found it benefited him from time to time.

He spoke six languages. Though, he knew Olive wasn't any less accomplished on that score.

"You often travel. I imagine your apartment is perfectly set up for you to leave at a moment's notice."

Her cheeks went red, and he could see that he was correct about that. And that it infuriated her.

Good.

"I don't have time to go anywhere with you. I have a project to work on."

"Then you didn't have time to betray me."

It was a strange word, that one. Betray.

They were enemies, or rather rivals, so perhaps it wasn't a betrayal at all.

Except… It was a betrayal of what he had thought she was.

And he did not like being wrong. In fact, he found it unacceptable.

"It is the principle of the thing," she said. "This. I can't believe that you wouldn't…"

"I wouldn't. If I had a tendency toward such things you would know it by now, Olive. I would've destroyed you that way. But I didn't. Because I do not do things like this."

They were silent the rest of the drive to the jet.

It was there, prepared and waiting, sleek and well appointed. He did all of his business in major cities, but Iceland would always be his home. Even if sometimes when he breathed too deep he felt like a shard of volcanic rock had lodged itself in his chest.

Even if, he could return to his homeland, but had never returned to his true home.

The house he kept now, tucked into the craggy mountains, just above a natural hot springs was his one refuge. He did not bring people there. Not women, not business associates. No one. It was in fact, almost entirely unknown, even by the media. And that was how he liked it. It would be the perfect place to spirit Olive away to, and have no one know where she had gone.

She was in the corner of the limo, wrapped in the blanket. "Must I drag you out of the car?"

"No," she said imperiously. She got out, still wrapped in the purple blanket, and thrust her nose into the air as she walked up the steps into the plane, looking every inch an indignant Queen.

He would say one thing for Olive, she had an exceptional amount of nerve.

She settled into the far corner of the plane, a couch the opposite end from him.

"It is a quick flight," he said. "It won't take long."

Takeoff was immediate, and once they had reached

altitude, he stood, and began to open up the drink cabinet. "Would you like something?"

"Obviously alcohol is off the table," she said.

"Obviously."

"I don't understand what you're doing," she said. "First of all, regardless of the paternity of the baby, you can't tell me that you actually want a kid?"

He looked at her, his blue eyes laser focused. "It is not about need. But we both need children, do we not?"

His own father had been a bastard. And as for the man who had been his father figure...

Gunnar had squandered that relationship. He had been wrong about what mattered. For it was not paternity. As for himself, he did not know how to be a father. But he did know that no child should be unwanted or uncared for.

He might not know how to show love or affection, but he had the means to care for a child.

"I suppose. To pass on the companies."

"It is why our fathers had us," he said. "Or at the very least, why my father decided to take part in raising me."

The words seemed to cut her beneath her skin. She flinched. "I suppose so."

"Anyway. I will let no child of mine go unclaimed. It is not my way."

"Oh, really? Is this not the first time for you?"

He ignored that.

"And what about you? You want a child?"

She shook her head. "I'm busy. But I have a lot of money, I imagine that nannies can... Handle everything. Otherwise, I happen to know that there's usually a good space for children to sit outside of conference rooms. And often there are snacks." Her voice wavered at the end, as if she heard the words she spoke, and realized what she was consigning a child to.

Their own childhoods. Repeating.

Neither of them spoke for a long moment, but they looked at each other, and he could feel the shared history between them. It was a strange thing. This.

For the most part, he felt connected to no one and nothing. He'd broken the happy home he'd once had with his idiotic, childish demands to be reunited with a father who hadn't loved him at all. He'd destroyed that connection. And as for his father...

Building one had never been on the table.

"Sometimes there are even cupcakes," she said, her voice a whisper now.

"Yes. I suppose there are."

They didn't speak after that. And he was perfectly fine with that. He was still volcanic with anger toward her. He had decided to ruin her, and now things were complicated. He resented this barrier to her ruination.

Ruthless? Perhaps. But he had only ever been taught one way to be. His father had taken a happy twelve-year-old boy and had broken him, remade him. Forged him in the fire of uncompromising fury, with yet one goal set before him. Winning.

Gunnar had taken all that fire and fury and used it to make his own path. Make himself his own man, apart from his father. He might be principled in a way his father never had been, but that didn't make him a man who knew how to bend.

Yet he'd grown too indulgent of Olive. He was reaping the punishment of that bad decision now.

He had seen her as soft. He had seen her as relatively harmless. He had seen her as something he wished to shield, protect. He did not need every contract in the tech market, and the fact was there were certain things that were better suited to the products that Ambient provided, than Magnum.

He was an honest man. To his core.

And perhaps that was what disappointed him so.

He had thought that she was better than her father. Better than his father. He had thought that she was…

He had respected her. He had, as far as his heart could care, cared for her.

And now, no more.

When his good opinion was destroyed, it could not be remade.

And she was potentially pregnant with his child. A fascinating and unwelcome turn of events.

And yet, the idea of her being pregnant by another man…

It ignited his blood. Made it run hot with fury.

And he did not know now which betrayal burned the worst. That she had proven herself to be dishonest in business, or that she was claiming she had given her body to another man after giving herself to him.

And he could feel the heartbeat of his ancestors in his chest as he imagined another man putting his hands on her skin.

She was looking at him, defiant.

Olive was a powerful woman. She went out of her way to never appear to be the sort of woman who used her sensuality to get ahead—and indeed, she did not use her sensuality in business.

It was a strange thing to think of other men seeing her as he did.

For he could not deny that he saw her as sensual.

And after being with her the way that he had been...

She was exquisite.

Her sexuality was a sweet, secret thing, a jewel at the heart of a steely reserve. One that you had to work to see—at least he had thought so. But she made it sound as if she gave her favors away freely.

He was surprised he had heard no rumors to that effect, but he could also imagine Olive going to great lengths to ensure that nobody knew.

To ensure that her brand of desire stayed under wraps.

For one thing he could appreciate about her. She had stepped into a man's world. All of the other CEOs of the major tech companies were men. Their fathers obviously had been.

And there was her. Groomed and trained to take over, certainly, but a woman all the same.

And he admired the way that she had fashioned for herself a niche.

She did not try to emulate the men around her. She did not wear suits. She did not try to borrow a masculine toughness.

But she had her own. Like a bright-eyed vole who kept her head down and scampered to glory.

She was…

She was a thief. Essentially. She had stolen information. She was not any of those admirable things that he had once imagined.

Just as her sexual favors clearly weren't rare or difficult to earn.

"If you think that I will be bringing you a steady supply of male concubines during your tenure at my residence, I will have to disappoint you."

"Drat. I absolutely do not know what I'll do without my concubines. I like to be fed grapes and fanned with palm fronds before I receive the evening's pleasure."

"Sadly. I am fresh out of grapes and palm fronds."

"Was that an offer of pleasure, Gunnar?"

The words held an edge, and he could see that she was attempting to mock him, but once their eyes met, heat flared there in the depths of hers, and her cheeks turned pink.

She was not as in control as she would like him to believe. And when he thought back to the entire actions of the day, from her clutching the crackers and behaving in such a ridiculous manner, to now, he could see that all of it was a wild attempt to keep him at arm's length. Because she had most certainly known that she was pregnant, whether she had taken a test or not.

And she did not want him to know.

Whatever she said, he had a feeling she was certain enough whose child she carried. He felt as if women generally did know such things. That even if they had multiple lovers, they often had suspicions. Her desperation to hide it from him gave him a fair idea of what her suspicions were.

"Was that an offer of pleasure?" She asked again, attempting to look bold.

"That all depends. I personally like a bit of pleasure with my pain. I'm not certain that you feel the same."

She shivered.

But he knew it wasn't from her lies or even fear.

Oh, yes. This was the problem. He had always sensed that little Olive was his match in a great many ways. In the bedroom, at least.

She had been asking him questions that were dangerous for him to answer with those wide beautiful eyes since she was far too young to be asking them.

After that exchange, Olive pretended to nap. She was not asleep, he was certain of that.

She was like a little kid, feigning sleep with her eyes scrunched tight.

He would've found it charming, if he were capable of finding her charming.

The plane landed on his private airfield, at the base of the mountain. The snow had begun to fall in earnest, capping craggy black rocks.

The house—made of concrete and thick glass—was nestled into the side of the mountain, all the better to shield it from the harsh weather.

The sea was to one side, the hot springs midway to the top of where the house sat.

All of it accessible only by tram.

He had one built specifically for the journey both to the hot springs, and the house.

They disembarked from the plane, and Olive looked around, her eyes wide. "Are we supposed to…walk?"

"Yes. I hope you brought your trekking poles."

"I didn't. And you well know I don't have a parka," she said, still wrapped in the blanket, standing out there with the vast expanse of snow behind her. She looked like a little drop of blood out there in the pristine wilderness, and he could not help but wonder if that were a metaphor of some kind. Certainly one he did not wish to examine too closely.

"I'm kidding."

"Are you capable of kidding?"

"Clearly. We take the tram to the top."

"What?" she asked, clearly not any more appeased by this than she was at the idea of walking.

"Yes," he said. "We take the tram to the top. It is quite nice. Beautiful view."

"I don't… That is…"

"Clearly you are not made of hearty Icelandic stock," he said.

"No. I am a city-dwelling marshmallow. This is… This is not… No."

But she was not about to freeze to death, and when he grabbed the edge of her blanket and began to tug her along, she came, taking tiny indignant steps as she endeavored to stay bundled up.

He took them to the edge of the tram platform, where the car was sitting. "It's probably cold in there," he said, not bothering to sound apologetic at all.

"Oh, gosh," she said, getting inside and shrinking into the corner.

She looked up ahead, her eyes round with worry.

"Are you afraid of heights?"

"No. I love them. It's a natural thing for human beings to love heights. What with how we are capable of gliding down safely if we fall from them."

"You're hysterical," he said, noting the genuine fear in her eyes.

He might have pitied her. But he knew her now.

"Thank you. I do try to keep some humor in these situations."

"No. That is not the kind of hysterical that I meant."

She looked up at him. "Really?"

"Do you see me laughing?"

"No. But then. I never have."

"Physically incapable," he said.

"Must be the Viking."

He shrugged. "Perhaps. Though Vikings had a particular affinity for me too. And I imagine if you get enough of it flowing through your veins a bit of pillaging seems amusing."

The car gave a jerk, and the cable began to carry them up the hill, up, up toward the mountain home.

And Olive became more and more agitated. The tram flew over the tops of the snowcapped trees, past rocky crags and waterfalls. And it was clear that at a certain point in spite of herself, Olive became too fascinated by the view to hide.

"It's beautiful," she said. "I can't believe I've never

been here. Of all the places in the world that I have been, I just… It's so strange…"

"Because the kind of business we do isn't done here. It's different. That's why it's my refuge."

"I don't have a refuge," she said. "New York born and raised. Unless we were in London. Or Tokyo. Or Berlin. Or Stockholm."

"It was a transient childhood for us both, I think."

"I consider myself lucky," she said. "Very few people have had the kind of on-the-job training that I had the opportunity to receive. Coupled with my experiences traveling… It doesn't get much better, I don't think."

He could remember time he'd spent in a small house. With a woman who had cared for him. A man who taught him about life, and not just business meetings.

He could remember real birthday parties. Evenings spent reading by the fire.

Olive had never had that. It made him almost find that pity for her again.

Almost.

One thing he knew, their child would not have an identical experience to them. And he would be sure of it. Their child would have a mother and a father.

He would marry Olive, and ensure that they had…

He thought again of the small cabin he had spent the first twelve years of his life in.

No. They would not have that.

But they would have something. They could not be people they weren't. And he had concerns about Olive and what she would teach a child.

But as long as she was bound to him, he could ensure it was all right.

"No. There is nothing better," he said.

"But I am glad to have seen this."

"Even though you're not very happy with me?"

"Well. I did not exactly anticipate that I would see Iceland on a nonconsensual vacation."

"A kidnapping?"

"No. You didn't kidnap me," she said.

"I think I have."

"Absolutely not. It's nothing more than a mandatory detour."

"Kidnap."

It took ten minutes for the cable car to reach the summit, and it stopped gently, letting them out at the automatic door to a long, heated corridor.

It was all glass, the windows looking out at the view on either side. "This is sort of terrifying," she said.

"It's beautiful," he returned.

"I guess. If you love heights."

"And I obviously do."

"Sure." She looked around. "So that is your game plan? Do you have a game plan?"

"You should know me well enough to know that I do. I will be finding out from a doctor how quickly we can get a paternity test."

"Oh."

"And the minute we discover if the baby is mine, you will marry me."

CHAPTER SEVEN

THE HOUSE WAS INCREDIBLE. Made mostly of glass with black window frames, concrete everywhere else, somehow light and airy rather than heavy or industrial as you would assume. Rather it made the house appear as if it was just another piece of the landscape. The windows offered a view of the sea, and the broad expanse of snowy wilderness on the other side.

And yet, it was difficult to concentrate on the beauty of the house what with the specter of a threatened marriage looming over her head.

"You cannot really mean that."

"I do. And for your sake, Olive, you had better hope the baby is mine. For if the child is mine, I will spare you time in prison, and I will have a care with Ambient, as it will be my child's legacy. Or rather, half of it."

"If the baby isn't yours then what? Then I'm hosed?"

"Emphatically."

"How can you…" She looked at him, at those eyes that were like ice chips, and she could see how well that worked as a comparison, since she was currently surrounded by ice.

And she had no idea what she had been thinking. Because she had in some ways not truly respected exactly who Gunnar was.

She had lied to herself about the level of comfort she could have in their… Relationship. Association. She had allowed herself to fashion him into a fantasy object that had blunted some of the truths about him.

He was a Viking. And she had betrayed him. Even if she weren't pretending she didn't know who the father of the baby was, spying on him, taking secrets from his company… Of course he took a dim view.

To say the least.

She should have listened to what he'd taught her the night they'd made love.

She had tried to control it, but Gunnar pushed the limits, found her true fantasies, her true self, beneath all the slick confidence she'd tried to convey.

Yet somehow she'd lied to herself. Convinced herself it wouldn't be that way outside of that experience.

She had let cupcakes and years together soften the reality of what she was doing to him. And the reality of what he would do in return.

And she had… She had been so caught up in her victory that she had underestimated fully the manner of predator that she had gone to bed with. And she had blocked out the lesson after.

She was an idiot. She was an absolute idiot. Well, more accurately, she was a mouse. And she was trapped handily beneath the paw of a lion.

She had a feeling no matter how she scrabbled or

scurried, she was going to stay exactly as she was. Trapped.

And so she would not debase herself.

"I'm tired," she said.

"Well, you are welcome to avail yourself to one of the bedrooms. Since your fake nap on the plane didn't actually gain you any rest."

"I challenge anyone to rest while you're looming about."

"I don't recall looming. I feel as if I was sitting."

"Of course. Nobody thinks that they loom."

"You say that definitively."

"I have a heavy exposure to men of all varieties, and believe me when I tell you, many of them loom, and none of them think they do."

"Go to sleep, Olive."

And she realized then that she was being left to her own devices.

She made her way down the hall, and opened a couple of different doors. All of the rooms were quite similar. Scandinavian sparse, with beds and fireplaces and sheepskin rugs. She chose the one with the purple bedspread. Simply because she had a bit of a theme going on.

And as soon as she closed the door, it was like layers upon layers of armor were peeling away from her body, and she had not given it permission to do that. She had cried at the clinic. But that had been different. It had still been controlled. She'd still been protected.

But just now, she felt as if she had been hollowed

out. As if there was nothing but misery contained inside of her.

Weakness.

A weakness that she strove always to hide.

A weakness she tried to ignore, but Gunnar had started to pick away at her defenses. When he'd brought up their childhood…

She wanted to howl, but she didn't. Instead she doubled over, a silent wail forcing her lips open, no sound coming out.

What had she done? A baby? She replayed everything that she had said to Gunnar over these past hours. The child could sit outside of conference rooms. Her childhood had been wonderful. Such an education. Traveling the world.

Lonely.

Lonely.

Lonely.

The honesty that lived beneath all those words assaulted her now.

She wanted to kick something. Wanted to rage.

Her childhood hadn't been wonderful. That thought made her feel like a terrible person. Like she was betraying the father who had raised her alone, the father she loved so much.

But it had been isolation. The reason that she had all these complicated feelings for Gunnar was that he was one of the only other human beings she knew. She didn't have friends. She had a… strange relationship with a man that she had a business rivalry with.

She was obsessed with him because she knew nothing and no one else.

Was this what she was consigning a child to? A life of… And what would she even have? Because Gunnar was now claiming he was going to take Ambient from her. And what would she do if she lost the company? Then all of her life, all of her childhood, all of the everything that she had ever worked for would mean nothing. Nothing.

She felt exhausted by her own misery. And she hadn't even fully given in to it yet. But it was like a living thing, digging its claws into her, and making her feel hopeless.

She didn't know who she was if she didn't have Ambient.

She didn't know who she was right now.

And she had no idea how to fix the mess that she had gotten herself into. She had never done a thing beyond what was expected of her. Not ever. Not once.

Until Gunnar. Until she had given in to the need that she felt for him, and look where she was now.

She was currently reaping a particularly awful harvest from a string of bad decisions.

The only bad decisions she had ever made.

And she had no idea how she was going to dig herself back out of this. None at all.

And so she surrendered to her misery. And she wept.

While Olive slept Gunnar was busy having items delivered for her. He also checked with the doctor who said that a blood test could ascertain the parentage of the child as soon as they could get it. And he made an appointment for the doctor to come to the top of the mountain as soon as he was able.

He also arranged to have a large spread of breakfast set out for the two of them. And then he slept for two hours.

He awoke before Olive, and just before the breakfast arrived. Baskets of breads and honey, dates and figs, and hard cheeses. The kind of breakfast you needed when you had been traveling and your body had no idea what time of day it was.

Olive's entire wardrobe arrived then as well.

He began to brew strong coffee, and it was then that Olive emerged.

In of course the same outfit she had on yesterday, her brown hair halfway released from its bun. Her eyes were swollen, her expression bleak.

"Good morning," he said.

"Good morning."

He wanted her. He realized that with a kick of lust and ferocity.

He wanted her. Even now, he wanted her. Even now, knowing how duplicitous she was.

He was a sick bastard, that there was something in that thought that actually made his desire kick up even higher.

He wanted to punish her.

Wanted to pin her down with his hand on her throat and make her beg him for mercy. And for pleasure.

There was certainly more of the old ways, and the old ancestors in his blood than he normally thought.

That, though, was nearly a comforting thought. It was the surge of tenderness on its heels that he felt desperate to deny. That he wanted to respond to her clear distress by wrapping her in a blanket, as he'd done the night of her father's funeral, and holding her close.

"Is it?"

"Morning?"

"Good," she fired back, looking angry.

He quite liked her angry. It was better than sad.

"You will be relieved to know that I have clothes for you."

"Wonderful. Did someone go and get my things?"

"No. I am tired of your self-imposed uniform. I would like to see you in some colors."

"Colors?"

"You wear all black. And I find it unbecoming."

"You found it becoming enough to screw my brains out a couple of months ago."

"Yes. But after I got you out of the clothes."

She huffed, and then looked hungrily at the spread set before them.

"This looks good."

"It isn't poisoned."

"How did you know that was the last question I was going to ask you?"

"Because smart-asses are predictable."

She wrinkled her nose. "Well, I'll get more creative then." He had a feeling that for Olive a lack of creativity was the singular greatest sin a person could commit. Which was yet another reason it was so odd that she had stolen from him the way that she had. For in his opinion it evinced an extreme lack of creativity. She must've been desperate. He wondered exactly why.

"Why did you do it?"

"What?"

"Why did you stoop so low to win that contract? It is not in your character, Olive, at least not in your character as I knew it."

She looked away. "I really needed to win that."

"And you possessed such little confidence in yourself?"

Her head snapped back, her eyes suddenly filled with anger. "No. That isn't it at all. It isn't that I had a lack of confidence in myself. I wanted to make sure. I think I would've won either way."

"And yet, you have no way of knowing. You stole not only from me, but from yourself."

"That's excellent, Gunnar. You should be a life coach. But this isn't inspirational Internet bullshit. I had to win."

"Yes. You've yet to give me a good reason why."

"Because it mattered to my father, and if it mattered to him, it mattered to me."

"Then why prolong it? Why go back to my penthouse? Why make the game into something sexual?"

"It wasn't the same thing. I wanted to win the contract for Dad." Her voice broke. "I wanted to do what he'd set me up to do, and I couldn't take a risk. You... You're a different part of that. I wanted you, and I... I needed to be done wanting you. I needed to be done being confused by you. I needed to be rid of you."

Her voice was low, trembling.

"It was so bad that you wanted me?" His voice was rough, almost a stranger's voice.

"Yes. I needed to be above it. Better than it. I hate that when I go into meetings I spent all of my time mentally undressing you. I just wanted it done. I wanted a clean break."

She cringed when she said the words.

"You're embarrassed about this?"

"Yes. Of course I am. Are you not embarrassed?"

"I don't spend any time being embarrassed of my inclinations. Whatever they may be. In life, things can be as simple or as complicated as you make them. For me, desire is a simple thing. If I want someone, I have them."

"So you had never wanted me before that moment I took my sweater off in your penthouse?"

It was a deliciously delivered barb, one that hit its mark.

Because she had in fact pegged him as a liar. She had been the one thing he had ever denied himself, and he had never really thought of it that way. He had never put it into words.

He was not a man given to self-denial or self-delusion, and the fact that he had such a blind spot there enraged him. Especially because she had called it out.

Had he ever wanted her?

It was such a complicated maelstrom of feeling. He could remember the first time he'd noticed the sweet lines of her body when she'd been eighteen, wrapped tightly in a black gown at a charity function, her lips painted red.

He could remember also, her being a sad, lonely-seeming child, and how he'd felt a strange mix of resentment and pity for her. Resentment because she was like an external echo of his own loneliness.

He could remember watching her give her first business presentation, being in opposition to her and wanting to protect her from failure all the same.

He could remember that pity and desire mingling when he'd held her after her father's funeral.

Had he ever wanted her?

It seemed so base to describe the way she'd gotten a hold on his soul all those years ago.

"I suppose," he said slowly, the words cutting his throat, "you intersect an uncomfortable line for me. I do not mix business and pleasure."

"Well, I was trying to disentangle those things. Get out from under the business, have the pleasure..."

"Why don't you sit down and eat. You look as if you're going to fall over, and I do not wish to be put in the position of having to cushion your fall again."

"What a trial for you."

But she came forward and began putting pastries on her plate. Along with honey and cheese. He brought her a mug of coffee. And when she took a sip, she smiled. "Oh, this is heaven."

"The doctor will be here today to administer a blood test," he said.

"What?"

"To determine whether or not the baby is mine."

She looked... Stricken.

"I didn't know you could do them this early."

"Yes. Blood tests have gotten very sophisticated."

"I hate getting my blood drawn. I hate it. It makes me pass out."

"Well, sadly for you, it is the way that they determine these kinds of things."

"The baby is yours," she said, staring fixedly down at her plate.

"What?"

"The baby is yours, I thought that I could... I thought I could get you to leave me alone if I told you I didn't know. I thought that I could..."

"You lied to me."

"I was freaking out," she said. "I don't know what to do. I don't know what to do. I've never slept with a man before, and I... I gave myself to you, and it was a very big mistake. I didn't think of protection, not at all, but you would think, that given that you are some kind of famed sex expert, that you would've thought to use condoms."

"Stop," he said, everything inside of him going quiet. "You've never been with a man before?"

"Well clearly I have been now," she said.

"You were a virgin." It was a roar of triumph in his blood, and he hated himself a bit for it. But he'd wanted her for so long, and to know she was his and his alone...

It made him feel every inch the conquering warrior.

"Yes," she said. "I was a virgin. Not that I care much about that kind of terminology. I knew what I was doing. I've read a lot of... I like books that have... Look, I know how everything works. So I was pretty well… Primed on the topic by the time I actually… I needed to get you out of my system."

"You're moving too quickly for me now. You know that the child is mine because you were a virgin."

"Yes. I don't need a blood test."

And he couldn't trust her. Or far worse, couldn't trust himself.

"Sadly for you, because the story keeps changing, now I require a blood test. Because I don't know which version of you is real, Olive. I always thought that you were my rival, but I felt that you were a rival that had a sense of integrity. And now I find out you have engaged in corporate espionage, and also, that you have lied to me. Either now, or before."

"Why the hell would I lie to you now? I would just tell you that I knew for sure the baby wasn't yours if I was lying. Because that would actually benefit me. I want to get away from you."

"It actually wouldn't benefit you. As I would see you in prison under those circumstances."

"I just… I don't… You're being ridiculous," she said.

"I'm being ridiculous?"

"Yes," she said. "I wouldn't lie to you about this. Not this time. Not now."

"You need to explain more clearly what led you to this point, because I have no idea what the matter is with you."

And then, all of a sudden, steely, tough Olive burst into tears.

CHAPTER EIGHT

SHE WAS DOING IT. She was losing her mind, and she was crying in front of this man. She didn't like it. Not one bit, but she couldn't stop herself. She was weeping, wailing. It was like she had lost all ability to be… Her. She had learned to be tough and strong and hold the shield up in front of all of her emotions when she was a girl.

A leader couldn't afford to be led by their feelings, her father had taught her that. Instilled it into her so deep it was like it was carved into her soul.

And now she was just… She was falling apart. Maybe it was the hormones. Did you already have those kinds of hormones at this point in the pregnancy? She didn't know. She didn't know anything about being pregnant. In many ways, she didn't know anything about being a woman.

She had no feminine influence in her life, she didn't really have any female friends. She saved all of her feminine feelings for fiction.

She identified heavily with the women in the romances that she read, and put herself in their place, and when she did that, she felt… whole in a way that she wasn't able to feel outside of that.

Because it was just so damned difficult.

Because in her real life she had to be unflappable, she had to be hard and she had to be capable of anything. And she did not feel capable of anything right now. In fact, she felt…

She felt like a disaster.

"I *needed* the contract," she said. "It was the one my dad wanted. It was in the portfolio as the single most important thing that he was working toward. But when I got in there and I saw the building blocks of what there was, of what he was working on a decade ago to go in these cars, once they were ready to go to market… It wasn't up to par. I had so much work to do so quickly. There was no real blueprint. But it was his white whale, and if I couldn't get it… If I couldn't get it, Gunnar, then I might as well not be in charge of the company. I might as well not be anything."

Admitting that to him made her feel so much shame. She wondered if Gunnar did anything to prove himself, or if he simply just did it. Because he wanted to. Because it was something that felt good to do.

This was the problem. It wasn't that for her. And it never could be.

"But what are you without your honor?"

"That's philosophical. A wonderful idea. You want to do things simply to prove you're the best. I wanted to do it to get the contract. It was something that mattered to my father. So how I did it didn't matter. It was just… The getting it." She squeezed her hands into fists. "It was the one thing he wanted of me Gunnar, and now it's ruined and gone. I was willing to debase myself, to violate any morals I might have to see this done, and it's for nothing anyway."

"I see. And where exactly does our passionate interlude in the penthouse come into play? Simply to get rid of me, as you've said before?"

She shook her head. "I did want that. Because you make me feel…a way I don't want to feel. But that night, I wanted something for myself. That's all. It was a mistake. Like everything else. I…" She felt small then. Utterly undone. "I'm not perfect." It cost her to say that. She looked up at him. "I'm not perfect. I don't know how to do everything. I have been trying as hard as I can to do everything that my father would've done, and sometimes I think I do better than him, and sometimes I think I… Sometimes I think I have no idea what I'm doing. And that's… That's all. But I wanted to win this. And then… I was weak, I guess. Across the board."

She watched his face as she admitted all this, tried to get a gauge for what he was thinking, feeling. She couldn't.

"You will do the blood test," he said.

"I don't…"

"You will," he said. "This is not up for debate or discussion. It is the way of things. And so, you will do as I say."

"You're such a dick," she said.

"And you have proven yourself to be duplicitous. Therefore, you will be punished for it."

"Punished with a blood test."

"With a lack of trust."

"What would I have to gain by lying now? I've ruined everything. Everything I cared about, it's all nothing, so you might as well know it all. I read Viking romance novels and fantasize about you carrying me off and ravishing me, I don't like the classics. I am in charge of this company, which I trained for all my life, and I feel unequal to it. All I wanted was to make my father proud and he died. He died and I didn't have a chance to show him, so I was trying to do it as an homage and I messed that up too, and now I'm pregnant, and yes, I lied to you. I was underhanded with the contract, I lied about being with other men, but I was trying so hard to protect myself, and now I can't so…why would I keep lying?"

She shrank beneath his withering blue gaze. And she found that she hated it. That she had earned his disdain. That she did not have his trust.

Why? Why did she feel this way for him?

He said nothing. He seemed unmoved by the way she'd just shattered, and it made her chest feel like it was too tight.

"Do you need to take everything from me, Gunnar, is that it?"

She had always known him to be steely, but he brought her cupcakes, and sometimes, it almost felt as if he were her friend as much as he was her enemy. She didn't have any others.

"If it seems I must."

In this, it he was proving that he was nothing like she had imagined.

She had thought that the hardness would give way to something else, because she felt sort of a connection to him.

But it was clear, he made it abundantly clear now, that he did not feel the same.

That underneath it all, he was the barbarian that she had fantasized about him being.

Of course, that had been in a sexual sense. And it was a lot more fun to imagine things in the bedroom, than spilling over into her actual life where there were real consequences and...

She supposed that was the issue. If you had fantasies about large, dominant men who made you feel small and beautiful and like they could scoop you up and handle everything, you had to take the negatives that came with that. Which in this case, turned out that he was a vindictive asshole.

Except... He wasn't acting like a child. He was not simply lashing out. It was all calm and measured. As if she were the child and this were the punishment that she deserved.

It got its hooks into her. Made her feel shame. Made her feel as if she were the foolish one.

As if she were the one that was small.

"Gunnar I..."

"You what? You vastly underestimated me. And that is the problem. You thought that because you won a few contracts when we went head to head that you knew the measure of me. But that is not the case, Olive. You do not know me. You do not know… You do not know what I thought of you before, and how this has changed things. And now you must face the consequences of your own actions."

"You act as if that hasn't been part of my life, all my life. You think my father was easy on me?"

She felt disloyal speaking of her father, particularly to Gunnar.

She loved her father. He was all she had. And she had loved him dearly. She also knew that essentially, Gunnar hated him, as his father had hated him. They had not had the type of rivalry that she and Gunnar had, where there was sniping but it was…

It was sexually charged. And you mistook it for something else.

Because for all your talk of reading romance novels and understanding the way of things, you were a silly virgin. And you did not protect yourself. At all. You are a silly, silly girl.

She felt silly. She felt absolutely foolish.

She felt as if she had completely ruined everything. Detonated a bomb in the middle of all of it.

She was so used to feeling like everything was well ordered, every risk calculated. And she had been so convinced that she had the measure of things, that she had moved forward with the corporate espionage. That she had moved forward with sleeping with Gunnar because she had found a way to make it all makes sense in her head. Perhaps that was the worst thing that her father had taught her. To trust in her mind.

In this case, she had managed to construct for herself a palace of nonsense.

And she couldn't live in that damned palace. No she could not. She was in Gunnar's ice palace.

But she had a feeling he was not going to let it go.

"My father expected me to be every inch the CEO that he was by the time I was twenty-two. He had all those years to become proficient at what he did, but he wanted me to step in to this company that he grew and have the lay of it. And yes, he had the skills to turn it into what it was, but he needed me to take the helm and do so with authority. I have never had another path. I've never had another option." She swallowed hard. "I had never had anyone else. I loved him, he loved me in his way, I know he did. I know he did. And all I have left is Ambient and it's the only way I can… I can keep on loving him."

"As you can see, my options were many and plentiful and laid out before me as the bounty of the earth." His tone was dry. His expression bland.

"I'm not saying you had it any differently. You are perhaps the only person in the entire world that understands exactly what it's like to be raised by a man like my father."

"I do not think that our fathers were the same."

"Don't you? I think they were. In essence. Certainly they did things differently, at least, in certain fashions. But… Don't you think… Don't you think?"

"I do not."

"Well. It doesn't matter whether you understand or not. I'm just explaining. If you want to try and find it in your concrete soul to empathize with what I was going through, you now have all the information."

"I don't do empathy."

"You did," she said. "You did when my father died."

"A mistake."

She continued eating, because it was only when she was eating that she did not feel like garbage. Either because of the pregnancy or because of the emotional duress that she was under.

And Gunnar sat unnervingly at the end of the table, palms flat, and it reminded her of the way he had stood in the penthouse that night. Regarding her, as she stripped her clothes off.

There was no way she could be feeling aroused by him. Not now. Not when he was being so… So awful.

But then, that was the way it was. Her attraction to him always and ever defied logic of any kind.

The fact that he was her most long-standing crush was just… *He is your only crush. Ever.*

And a man less deserving of a title of childhood crush, she could not think of.

He was not a pop star. No smooth boy-band member who might make a young girl comfortable. No. She had always been swinging above her weight class. Always.

Maybe that was part of what had been instilled in her. Maybe that was why she had never been able to find it in herself to be interested in a man who was less confronting.

Because it was all about Gunnar. Beginning and end of story.

Because she had been taught to be ruthless, efficient, and above all else goal oriented. And a man who seemed like he could be anything less wouldn't appeal.

She was such a mess.

And she was pregnant. With this man's baby.

And suddenly, she felt as if the entire world had shifted.

She really hadn't had time to wrap her brain about any of this. She had been caught up in trying to keep Gunnar from knowing the truth. She hadn't really examined what it meant that she was having a baby.

Was she really going to have that child sit outside of boardrooms?

She knew how to be a CEO. It had been what she was trained for.

She wanted to have a moment of knowing what it was like to be a lover. Because it had been exhilarating. Because it had been freeing in a way. To embrace her femininity in a fashion that she had never done before.

She wanted that. But then… Now she was going to be a mother.

A mother.

She hadn't even had a mother, she had no idea how to be one. She only knew how to be one thing.

And raising a child was all expansive, it required you to shift yourself, change yourself, wrap yourself around them in protection.

No one ever did that for you.

No. But the idea of bringing a little life into this world and not doing that… It seemed almost untenable. How could she? How could she give a child exactly the same life that she'd had when she stood here at twenty-six knowing how incapable she was of living in any other part of the world?

She knew her office. A corner office with a fabulous view, and she certainly had money and assets enough to take care of her basic needs. But she did not have friends, she didn't know how to be with a man... She didn't know... And he wanted to get married.

Suddenly, she wanted to cast up her accounts.

But she didn't want to do that, because it would be humiliating.

And she just couldn't bear any more humiliation. Not in front of Gunnar.

"Are you well?"

She shot him her most deadly glare. Her CEO face. "No. I'm not well. I'm pregnant."

"Silly question, perhaps."

"Let me ask you this. What are your plans for a child?"

He looked at her. "The child will be my heir."

"You certainly don't plan on arranging anything emotionally around the life of the child."

"Do you?"

"Do you expect me to? Because I'm the woman?"

"Yes," he said. "I do."

"What a relic."

"I also expect you to because your workload will be drastically reduced as acting figurehead of a company that I will now be in charge of. So it has less to do with your gender and more to do with the fact that you will be significantly reduced."

"How can you... How dare you. It isn't your company. You're not the one that built it. You're not the one that gave up… Childhood. You're not the one that gave up friendships and parties and sex, to run it."

"I think you'll find that I managed to work sex into my schedule."

"You're a man," she said. "You're a man, and people will expect it of you. People are fine with you sleeping around, but you tell me, who am I supposed to sleep with? Perhaps you're comfortable giving yourself to some empty-headed model to fill the hours, but I cannot respect a man who isn't as smart as I am. Who isn't as driven as I am. And if I can't respect a man… I don't want to sleep with him. Also, you men… You're idiots. I'm sorry. Women are the ones who must risk actual death to sleep with a stranger. Not only that, we are not guaranteed satisfaction. The risk is greater. And therefore, I find myself unwilling to take it."

"And that is why you were a virgin?"

"Yes," she said, "that's why."

Easier than admitting that he was the only man she had ever wanted, and the only man that she could imagine wanting, because that was just a horror.

"Well. We will see soon enough if that is true."

"It was true. I mean, I'm flattered that you think that I had a comprehensive enough set of skills to believe that I had a parade of lovers before you, but sadly, no parade. I am the grand marshal of my sexual parade of one. So."

"Extremely vivid. But then, you always did have a way with words."

"Indeed."

"Well, I eagerly await the news from the doctor. We shall see what his report is."

"Great."

"And then…"

"Yes. I know. Ruination. Marriage."

"In the meantime, have another doughnut."

"You know. I might as well."

And she realized then that she had been eating as if this were her last meal.

As if she were a prisoner bound for execution. She felt very like she might be.

For Gunnar was her Viking captor, and whatever lay ahead was not in her control.

CHAPTER NINE

WHEN THE DOCTOR ARRIVED, Olive swept out of her room wearing a camel-colored sweater and loose white pants that flowed with her every motion.

She looked soft, her dark hair down and framing her face. Markedly different to the woman she typically was, in her black uniform.

"I see you have rejuvenated."

"As much as possible. Though, I am a bit chagrined to see there is no black."

"None," he said grinning.

"That seems mean. Unnecessarily."

"I feel that you are mean to yourself, unnecessarily."

She mused on that. "I'm not mean. It is simplification. Also, I have never seen fit to dress for the approval of others."

She was beautiful all the same. Though he did not say so.

He found that he should be more disdainful of her than he was.

He of course had to give a blood sample as well, to determine the match. The doctor gave her a general once-over for her health as well.

"I will call you with the results," the man said.

Olive was pale and mute following the blood draw, and she curled up on one of his white couches, next to the roaring glass-backed fireplace that offered a view of the valley below.

"I'm tired," she said, resting her cheek on her forearm, which was leaned against the back of the couch.

"Yes. I can see that. How exactly do you suppose you're going to take on this business project while this exhausted."

"I have done some googling," she said. "I should only be this tired for the first trimester. Anyway, I only have four weeks left of that."

"A boon for you, then."

"Oh, yes," she said. "I'm in the middle of a huge boon. Truly, I have never been so boon to."

"Perhaps you need help. Perhaps, my acquisition of Ambient will be beneficial to you."

"Somehow, I don't think so. Somehow, I think you're trying to position a hostile takeover as a favor, and I find that to be disingenuous, and frankly, think you're better than that."

"Fine. Do you want honesty? I find you unworthy of retaining ownership of your company. After that stunt that you pulled."

"Unworthy. Gunnar finds me unworthy. Whatever shall I do?"

"Begin to make your apologies, Olive."

"Screw your apologies."

"You are unrepentant?"

"I think I've made that quite clear."

"You'll find that I am also unrepentant. Whatever happens after this."

She faced him down, her hazel eyes glittering. "Tell me this, Gunnar. Would you have brought me up here if I weren't pregnant?"

He shook his head. "No. I would have had you arrested and dealt with the fine details later. While taking over your company."

"Why did Jason tell you what I did?"

"I think he hoped that he might find himself on the receiving end of a promotion. For his honesty. He decided to manipulate you instead of me. And... That is his prerogative. Though, it did not end the way that he had hoped."

"You didn't reward him for his loyalty?"

"He was duplicitous. Both to me and to you. There is no honor among thieves, as such. At least you have loyalty, Olive. I find your moral compass to be skewed, but your loyalty is to your company. To the vision that your father laid out. That is a fixed loyalty. It makes sense. It can be tracked. Someone who is continually changing the guard as it were, is not trustworthy in any fashion."

She sniffed. "I suppose at least there's that. He's a bigger rat than I am."

"So you admit that what you did was wrong?"

"Why is it so important to you that I admit it? I'm not certain that it's wrong, if there's a weakness in your system. Again, we have different goals. Mine was to get the contract. Yours is to feel a certain way about how you go about getting the work."

"And why does it not matter to you?"

"Because I have to… Like I told you. I have nothing. I am nothing apart from this. You have this whole other company that you've built. I have this one thing. And I was willing to try and get whatever I could from you at all costs. Because it just seemed… It seemed reasonable. At the time."

And he could see, unspoken, that nothing much seemed reasonable now. Now that she was pregnant with his child.

You believe her?

He looked at the sad, waifish creature sitting before him. He would never have thought of Olive as *waifish* before. But yes. He did believe her.

Though this was just another way in which he'd failed to see Olive, when he'd been so convinced before that he had.

That she was a virgin was difficult to wrap his mind around, because she was a beautiful woman, and confident, determined.

But there had been clues. She did not seem to care about her appearance—though he had been certain enough that she would be able to get whatever man she might wish to have.

She clearly did not think so, though. She felt that she needed to stay buried in work, and work alone.

He wondered if that was how her perspective had become so twisted.

As if yours is better?

Yes. It was better. He did not have a more emotional life than she did, but he had honor. He might not believe in things like love, and he himself might not have friends, but he lived by a specific code.

Which was why it disgusted him so when he flared in his midsection when he looked at her.

He should not find her half so compelling. Not now. Not after everything.

And yet he did.

"Are you hungry?"

"Assume that I'm hungry unless stated otherwise," she said.

"But you don't seem to feel well."

"If I'm eating it makes it bearable. Strange, I know, but I didn't know anything about this sort of thing… And I don't really know what's normal and what's not, but that seems to be the way of things for me."

He went to the fridge, and took out a large tray of meat and cheese. She looked at him with skepticism. "Why are you being nice to me?"

"Do you consider this nice?"

She blinked, and tilted her head, and she looked rather like a questioning sparrow. "I… Well, I don't really know. Maybe it isn't all that nice. I don't have a lot of interaction with people. I have employees. And I have…" She started laughing. "I have you. I have you, and we spar and fight, and you bring me cupcakes. I guess you like to feed me."

"It was a game," he said.

"Well, you are the only person that I play games with. I think I sadly misread what we were."

"What exactly did you think?"

"I would've said that you were my rival. My enemy. But sometimes I felt as if you were my only friend."

"I do not have friends," he said. She nodded slowly, the desolation in her eyes puncturing something in his chest.

"No. Of course you don't. You are... You're a Viking. A warrior in all things. A man with a code of honor, but..."

"There is no point bringing emotion into anything," he said.

"Well. That's a lie. You're entirely comfortable with anger, which as far as I can tell is essential to men."

Anger.

The truth of that was a scalding handful of ash pressed hard into his chest.

"Anger is the one emotion that can exist unfettered," he said. "Anger is clear."

"You get so angry with me for having been dishonest, but you are lying to yourself. It's just... It's an emotion loophole. You're not cold if you're angry. Not at all."

"You speak very confidently of things you do not know," he said.

She waved a hand. "I know well enough. We watched each other become who we are now."

"Yes. I suppose that is true."

"I always thought that you brought me cupcakes because you felt bad about taking that last one. Since it was my birthday."

"I didn't know it was your birthday."

"I didn't mention it."

"But you did mention the cupcake often enough."

"Well, then you started bringing them to me. So it worked."

"You started craving chocolate the minute you heard my footsteps. Which was more my aim. I found it amusing."

"Yes. You trained my body to respond to you."

Suddenly, it was as if she heard the words after they exited her mouth, and she breathed in sharply, her eyes going round.

"Indeed."

"Well. Hopefully the doctor calls soon. So we can get down to the rest of your threats."

"You are looking forward to them?"

"What other choice do I have?"

But he could see that there was calculation behind her eyes. Because she was not weak. He could not afford to get caught up in her again. She was a worthy opponent, and he had to not forget that.

CHAPTER TEN

APPARENTLY, IT TOOK a little while to get the results on a DNA test. And Olive was doing her best to pass the time until Gunnar confirmed what she suspected they both already knew.

After breakfast that morning she explored. Every room in the house was a particular sort of beige, not plain, just tranquil.

But then she opened the door at the back of the house, and was stunned by a riot of color. The shelves were lined with action figures, still in their boxes, stacks of board games and bins of… Candy.

"What?"

"What are you doing in here?"

She turned to face him, her heart pounding rapidly. "I was only… I just wanted to look around."

"And now you have."

"What is this?"

His face went hard. "It is nothing."

"It's not nothing. Look at all these toys…"

"It is a collection," he said.

"Surely candy is not part of the collection." She examined the rows of sweets. All brightly colored and very out of character.

But then, he'd eaten her cupcake.

Maybe it wasn't out of character.

"In a manner of speaking it is."

"You don't eat the candy?" she pressed.

"I do," he said.

And she might have laughed, at the discomfort she saw in him just now, except she could sense something vibrating beneath the surface, and it concerned her.

"Why?"

"It started as collecting some things I had when I was a child, and it expanded. Every billionaire must have a prescribed amount of novelty items that make no sense. I am quite a bit under the usual threshold."

"That is fair. You don't have an entire fleet of electric cars."

"Only three."

"Well, there you are. You are actually quite restrained." She moved further into the room, her hands brushing up against one of the games. "Do you play these?"

"I've never had anyone to play with."

She looked at him, and she felt…

It was such a tangle of emotions. Because he'd brought her here, and threatened her business, and turned her life upside down. And he was also…

Him. The him he'd always been. Who bewitched her and tangled her up, and made her want things she'd been certain she could never have.

Who vexed her and charmed her sometimes in equal measure. Though usually he was more vexing.

He was a cold, forbidding Viking warrior.

A man incensed by her lack of honor.

A man who had kissed her like he'd die if he didn't have her.

A man who had this room, hidden away in the back of his house.

"Gunnar. We have to play a game." She took the box off the top of the stack, one she was familiar with. A strategy game that was all about building empires with wheat and sheep and ore. "We must not pass up this opportunity to match wits with one another."

"Must we not?"

"Absolutely."

"I suppose while we are still waiting for the doctor…"

In truth, she was just desperate to have a moment with him that wasn't…well that wasn't fraught or angry.

"Yes. All right."

He took the game from her hands and walked out of the room, charging toward the kitchen. She followed. She sat across from him at the table, and it quite reminded her of times they had sparred in the boardroom. They set up their game tiles and chose their pieces.

"You should fear me. I am a master at this kind of thing," she said.

And he smiled at her. For the first time in a long while. "You should fear me. I am a Viking."

She smiled back. "Oh, I know."

They got stuck into their gameplay, and it was fearsome. And there was something about the moment, about the connection. Him smiling and laughing when he would rob her of her land, that made the time fall away. And she wished they could've done this before. She wished they could've been children together. Properly.

She wished that things could be different.

He was another side to the coin of her existence. There was no one else like him. Nobody. And she feared if she couldn't find a way to connect with him, to fix this with him, she would never have a connection with anyone.

"I'm quickly cornering the market on sheep," he said.

"I'm not sure that's something to be proud of," she said.

"I think you will find that it is."

He grinned, the way he did when he presented her with a cupcake.

"You know what you were doing with the cupcake," she said. And to his credit, he did not seem confused at the abrupt introduction of the subject. It was almost as if he had been thinking of it too.

"You mean I knew I was training you?" He shrugged. "Perhaps."

"I've never understood it, you know. What we were. Really. Before all this. Before I… Before I broke it with what I did. And I am sorry. I am. And then we made a muddle of it with sex and then… Here we are. I never understood."

"We are not like anything else," he said.

And that, she feared, was the only answer to be had. They were not like anything else.

They had not quite been friends, but never quite enemies. Rivals, but allies in some ways.

It had all gotten strained and difficult with her attraction to him. With the way the loss of her father had spurred her to behave.

She felt so much loyalty to her father, but sometimes she wasn't sure why. More and more there were cracks beginning to form, particularly if she imagined what kind of parent she might want to be. Particularly if she imagined what her life might look like going forward. And in those moments of honesty, she could realize that Gunnar had actually been the closest person in her life. The one who had been the most human on many different occasions.

"You're right," she said. "We're not like anything else."

Tension stretched between them, and what she really wanted to do was close the distance between them and kiss him. What she really wanted to do was take back so many of the things that had happened in the last couple of months. Just so she could erase the anger that he felt at her. The obvious betrayal it had created.

"Did I hurt you?" she asked.

His eyes suddenly turned into ice chips. "No. You do not have the power to do such a thing."

"Oh. It's only that… You have been very angry at me."

"Yes. I have been."

"But?"

"You do not possess the ability to hurt me, Olive."

And she could hear beneath that, a firm *no one does*.

"And so now you won't take my word. You won't take my word that the baby is yours."

"Just play the game, Olive."

"Or is waiting for the test results just a bit to punish me."

"I do not need to punish you."

"All right then, is marriage not meant to be a punishment?"

"It is meant to be a solution."

"All right. So tell me, will we ever be friends again?"

"We were never truly friends to begin with."

"So you'll tell me that I'm singular, unique. That we are like nothing, but you cannot tell me that we are friends?"

He shrugged. "I don't have friends."

She gestured to the board game. "This is a very odd way of expressing it."

"I have colleagues, I have lovers."

"And you intend to take me as a wife. I already know what the results will be. So I already know what you will demand. And so I want to know. What does it mean? Will you love the baby? Will you ever love me?"

She felt small and afraid asking that question, and she did not wish to know why it affected her so.

His expression went flat. "There is no love left in me."

"Then what's the point?"

"Sometimes the point, Olive, is to simply do the right thing."

"What if the right thing becomes the wrong thing if there's no feeling behind it?"

"It does not matter if the end result is the same."

"I think it does," she said.

"Then you are free to feel as you see fit."

"I won," she said. "And I didn't cheat." She looked at the board game and counted up her resources.

He frowned. "So you did. You're a worthy opponent."

And he got up and walked away, without speaking. And she wished, more than anything, that she could find a way to be something to him other than an opponent, worthy or not. She wished that she… She didn't wholly know what she wanted from Gunnar. Or perhaps she was simply afraid to put voice to it.

They were *them*. Like nothing else. This had reminded her of that period of their long history. Of the years that had not been this. This fraught, terrible thing. But the last few months could not be altered or changed. They had to find a new way to be.

And she ached. With wanting him. Not just physically but… She wanted to piece back together the emotions.

But tomorrow the test results are going to come back, and they are going to be positive. And he's going to marry you. That grim man who hates you now so very much.

And it was a long future that stretched before her, married to that man. One that reminded her far too much of the cold in her childhood.

She was going to have to come up with a plan, because she did not think she could bear it.

She'd already had a lifetime in offices, with no birthday parties. She could not philosophically consign herself to more of the same.

CHAPTER ELEVEN

OLIVE KNEW IF she was going to escape, it had to be tonight.

This wasn't going to work. He was so angry with her, with everything, and so convinced of his rightness. She'd tried connecting with him, tried to find their footing and he'd closed it all down.

He had said he'd never love her.

And she just needed…

She needed some control back. She'd given it all to him when she'd told him there had been no one else, no other men. That the baby was his and she'd loved her father and she was broken by his loss.

That she'd wanted Gunnar as a gift for herself. She'd told him that.

She felt unmade.

Unraveled.

Her father had told her never to fall apart like this. To never let her emotions cloud her judgment. To never let them take the lead.

And here she was.

She needed to regroup. She could not let him take

control of her. She could not be…here with him, she just needed space to sort it all out.

And maybe part of her just couldn't accept allowing him to win.

He wanted her here. Wanted to marry her. Wanted her on his turf.

Or maybe you just don't want to be with someone else who looks at you like you're a disappointment…

She shut that thought down.

Yes, her father had sometimes treated her like she might disappoint him. Yes, that had hurt. But daddy issues weren't the thing here. Maybe. Probably.

Handily, in her new clothing, he had included clothes with which to make a track in this sort of weather. She still had her phone, though, and she had managed to charter herself a private jet, which would land soon enough, some distance away from his home. The airstrip there was private, and the pilot had been adamant that he could not land on it without permission from the owner, which was going to be a problem, since she needed the owner to not know that she was fleeing. It would sort of undermine her escape if he knew.

At midnight, with the snow falling softly outside, she put on the fur-lined leather pants, boots and parka that he had provided for her. And then she slipped from the bedroom, ready to make her way down the hall.

She was not going to keep him from coming after her forever, but she didn't have to be secluded in his mountaintop retreat.

She was going to get back on her own turf, get her

lawyers involved, get into a position where she could attempt to defend her business.

Attempt to defend herself.

He could not force her down the aisle, after all. If he was intent on ruining her either way…

This was the thing. If he did not have her, he would have to negotiate. And she needed to put Gunnar in a position where he had to negotiate.

He would have to give a forfeit of some kind. If he was holding her bodily against her will, then she became the token.

And she did not wish to be the token. So, she would not be.

Keeping her footsteps silent, she slipped through the living room area, and to the corridor that led to the sky tram.

Of course, it was only when she arrived at the sky tram that she had the thought that she actually had no idea how to run the sky tram.

She looked for a box and tried to figure it out. Look for controls. She couldn't see anything. It was dark, and the snow was coming down thick.

But that was okay. She was intrepid. She knew exactly how they had gotten up, it was a straight line. And so, she decided to head down on foot. She knew that it would be a bit of a long walk, but thankfully she was outfitted. She was prepared.

She moved her foot to a rocky outcropping, and slipped. She clung tightly to the ground, the frozen dirt biting into her fingertips.

No. She would be fine. She wasn't going to give in.

She wasn't going to turn back. She was just going to go step by step down the mountain. Because it was the only way down.

Just step by step. And she would make it.

She had to.

For herself. For the baby.

She would.

He woke up when he heard a noise.

He got up, and dressed—he always slept naked—and went outside. He didn't see anything. And then he went to Olive's room, and found her bed abandoned.

Her phone was gone.

Of course. Whatever she was doing…

She was not trustworthy. Not on the level that he would've liked her to be.

But what did she think she was playing at? If she went out there in the dead of night she was going to die.

And the baby…

He growled, throwing on his winter clothes and grabbing a stack of blankets.

He saw that the tram was still in place, and judging by the way the snow was situated on it, it had not moved. But of course, there would be no way she could operate it.

Had the little idiot actually gone down the mountain on her own?

He growled in a fury, and began to go after her.

She could only be a few minutes ahead.

He tried to find her through the thick sleet, but didn't see her.

He hiked down in a straight line, making it halfway down the mountain without ever seeing her once. And he knew beyond a shadow of a doubt that she had not gone that far ahead. She had to be lost. She was zigzagging, or she had taken a wrong turn.

Perhaps she was parallel to him.

But he could not imagine that she had made as much progress down the mountain as he had. It was familiar to him, and he knew where he was going. She did not.

He turned and started to go back up the mountain, keeping his eyes to the left and right. And after a fashion, he simply began to call for her. "Olive," he said. "Olive."

And then he saw her. With three inches of snow built up on her coat, crouched down against the side of the mountain. Her eyes were closed, her body limp.

"No," he said, his voice rough. He went to her quickly, shaking her. Her head lolled back and forth, and her eyes opened, dazed.

"You little idiot," he said.

"You're not the pilot."

"Fool," he said.

And he began to beat a path as quickly as possible to the hot springs. It was shielded from the wind and snow, and it was much closer than the house. He needed to warm her up, and he needed to do it quickly.

When they arrived at the edge of the hot springs he set her down in the snow, and stripped himself naked with ruthless efficiency, then he picked her up, and did the same to her, carrying her into the steaming pale blue liquid. She didn't rouse when the hot water touched her skin. Her lips were tinged blue, and he cursed. He can only hope that hypothermia had not set in in truth, or she would be in much bigger trouble than a hot springs would be able to solve.

He moved the water over her skin, and ignored the stirring in his body.

She was beautiful, it was true, and he had been battling attraction for her along with his anger these past few days, but now was not the time.

Her eyelids fluttered open. "Oh," she said, thrashing suddenly in his arms.

He held her tight up against his chest, her hands splayed there. "Settle down," he said.

"What happened? Where am I?"

"You're in the hot springs."

"I'm not supposed to submerge in water over a hundred and four degrees. I read that online when I couldn't sleep the other night."

"You probably aren't supposed to freeze either. But don't worry, the water isn't even one hundred degrees."

"Where am I?"

"Three-quarters of the way down the mountain. I found you on an outcropping. Because you nearly killed yourself doing whatever the hell you were trying to do. Which makes your lectures about water temperature feel a bit empty."

Her eyes went wide. "I *did*?"

"Yes. What were you playing at?"

"Escaping, obviously. But I figured it was a straight shot down the mountain…"

"And you managed to get yourself going sideways.

It doesn't matter, I don't think you would've made it to the bottom. You're small, and you don't move quick enough. I think you do not have an adequate understanding of how cold it is. You've been out here now for a couple of hours."

"I have been?"

"Yes. You might not want to believe me, but you should. I wouldn't lie to you."

"Right. Because of your honor."

"I have no need to. I have been up-front with you about who I was and what I was doing from the beginning. You know better."

She trembled in his arms, and he thought perhaps now might not be the time to yell at her. But she was an idiot. And she deserved it.

"Did I really nearly get myself killed?"

"Yes. You have got to stop acting as if you can overcome anything. You cannot overcome winter."

"I just… I've had to train to be in charge. To handle everything. I don't have the luxury of being tentative. I don't have the luxury of… You know that. You know how it is."

"You cannot wage war against temperature. It does not matter how determined you are. It does not care how brilliant you are. The weather will equalize you. To everyone else."

"I have a pilot coming."

"Stupid girl," he said. "No pilot can land in this. Even if a pilot said he was coming, he is not coming now."

"Really?"

"Yes. You might've traveled the world, but you certainly don't have an adequate respect for the kind of snow we get here. The kind of cold. Children here learn, and early, that they must have a care for the wilderness. For the turn in the weather."

His grandfather had taught him how to respect the wilderness and all the creatures in it. To love the cold, even as he respected it. He had taught him that the earth was living, and like any living being it had to be respected.

He carried that with him. Always.

"How are we going to get out of this without freezing to death?"

"Getting out will be unpleasant. But it will help that you warmed up. And I brought blankets."

"Did you know that I wouldn't make it?"

"I didn't stop to think," he said.

"I thought that I would make it," she said.

"Yes. I realize that." He snorted. "I did not think that you were suicidal over the prospect of marrying me."

"No. I wanted leverage."

And suddenly, it was as if she became conscious of the friction between their bodies. Of the fact that there was no clothing between them. Her cheeks went pink, and she wiggled slightly.

"What kind of leverage did you want?"

"What I wanted," she said, "was something. Anything. As long as you're holding me, you're holding all the cards, aren't you?"

"I have not offered you a buffet, Olive. This is not a chance for you to choose what you would like and put back what you do not. This is not an endless array of options for you. You have left yourself little choice here. You have no one to blame but yourself."

"Now, on that score you're wrong. The pregnancy was not just me. So don't be like that."

"All right. I will give you that. You are not alone in that."

"Oh. I know. I remember. I remember your…" She wiggled slightly. "Your involvement."

"A delicate way of putting it," he said.

"Well. I'm nothing if not delicate."

"Do not do anything so foolish again," he said, smoothing his thumb over her cheek. She looked improbably young, and he could remember when she had been a girl. And a wild one at that. He remembered when she had been as vulnerable as she looked now, and he wondered if anyone had ever held her then. He just wondered. He did not think they had.

And he should not feel any sympathy for her. Her choices were hers, and hers alone. As his had been. He had no sympathy for himself either. He had chosen to leave this place, to leave the people who had loved him. He had chosen to go with his father. He had been wrong about his father, and the consequences of that had been his to bear.

As her consequences were hers.

She might have felt some pressure from her father but the man was dead. He could not actually force her to do anything. He could not influence her.

At some point, everyone had to stand on their own feet and own who they were. What they were.

"You are warm," he said, his voice coming out rougher than he intended.

"Yes," she said.

"Let us get you back to the house. Do not try anything like this again."

"Not in the snowstorm."

"Never," he said.

"I'm not a kitten, Gunnar. I am not the kind of person who is simply going to lay down and accept what you have decreed. I am a woman. A woman who has been taught how to fight. I'm hardly going to let go of that now."

"The war is over. Consider yourself pillaged."

"The war isn't over until you're dead. And even then… I'm pretty sure that I would haunt your ass."

He chuckled. He couldn't help himself. It was the absurdity of it. Of her spirit. From the moment he had found her crouched behind her desk eating crackers. And she had tried to play it off. She never admitted when she didn't have the upper hand. But sadly for her. Sadly for her, she was the decisive loser in this battle.

He reached to the banks of the hot springs and laid out one of the blankets, then he lifted her from the water and set her on the blanket. She grabbed one of the folded blankets and wrapped it around her body. The dim light and her quick concealing of her curves made it so he didn't get a good look at her body. For the best, he supposed.

Then he got out of the water, his feet planted in the snow, and he dried himself quickly with the remaining blanket, before dressing quickly. Then he set about to help her get dressed without letting too much of her body be exposed to the cold.

He realized then that she was staring, wide-eyed.

"Yes?"

"Well, I'm never going to be used to just… You being naked. But also… Are you made of ice?"

"No but there is a resistance. Or perhaps I have a comfortable relationship with it."

"I have a comfortable relationship with fuzzy blankets."

"Women who are half so attached to blankets should not go taking off in the blizzards."

"Well, maybe if women who are attached to blankets were not also attached to freedom and agency, they wouldn't."

"Maybe those women who like blankets, freedom, and their agency, should not commit corporate espionage."

"Maybe men who are made of ice shouldn't be such sore losers."

"Again. Was I a loser?" he pressed. "Or did you cheat."

"Functionally immaterial to me."

"So you said."

When she was finished dressing, he looked up the side of the mountain. Thankfully, the snow had let up. "Climb on my back."

"What?"

"I'm going to carry you up."

"No. No. You don't need to do… No."

"Are you through arguing with me?"

"Yes," she said, exasperated as she hopped up onto his back, her legs resting on his lean hips, her arms around his throat. The softness of her body pressed against his sent a lick of heat through him. How was it she did this to him? After what she'd done. After running away. After all of it. How did he still want her like this?

"This is kind of dumb," she said. "Because I could strangle you if I wanted to."

"And how would you get yourself off the mountain."

"All right. That is a serious concern."

She was silent for a while.

"I really did think I could get myself out of this with sheer determination. That's what my father taught me, you know. Dad always said separating a person from greatness was their own unwillingness to be uncomfortable. That you had to work hard in order to achieve things, and… Once I realized that all of it was in my control… I've had a hard time doing things any differently. I mean, if it's just temporary discomfort… Why not push through? That was what propelled me down the mountain tonight. Cold is just temporary discomfort."

"Temporary discomfort that can kill you."

"I don't look at it that way. I didn't. I'm just trying to explain. All these things. The long work hours, the not having relationships, the… The corporate espionage even. They are unfortunate accessories to the main goal. And what my dad taught me was that the ends always justify the means. They always do. All you have to do is… Just ignore all the things that you need."

Her words tapered off on that last sentence. As if she suddenly heard what she had said. "The problem is, it never ends. You never arrive at a point where you go… Well. That's enough. It's sufficient sacrifice. No. I haven't found that yet. It's like you get to a point and you think… That wasn't so bad. I can keep going. I can do it again. I can… I can keep pushing myself. I'll catch up on sleep later. I'll make friends later. I'll have a relationship later. And you just chip away at yourself. At who you are and what you expect. At what you think you deserve. Until… Until it's only work. Until it's only work and you don't remember anymore what it's like to be something other than a robot." She tightened her grip on him. "I never set out to be a robot. I just wanted to make him proud. I just loved him and I wanted to be…what he wanted me to be."

He'd wanted that from his father once. He knew what it was like to not see. To not know.

"And I just took one little thing for myself," she whispered.

"That night in the penthouse was your indulgence?"

Except it had been his too. Whether he wished to admit it or not. She had been off-limits for a very long time, and few things were off-limits to him. He set the parameters for his life, and if he wanted something, he usually took it. But not her. For very specific reasons, not her.

He made sure to act dutifully as a better man than his father. But he'd had no confidence he could be better for her truly.

But he'd broken that rule.

And the world had come crashing down on him.

He was an Icelander to his soul. Protecting the land, the natural resources mattered to him more than just about anything.

And he tried to have harmony in all parts of his life. His business life did not conflict with the morals he felt outside of it.

And yet, he had to wonder at the exacting symmetry of all these things.

For it was more as if he had no other life at all.

Olive seemed to be at war. With what she wanted, with who she was. With what she did.

She was a fascinating constellation of fractured stars. Little things here and there that seemed to speak of dissonance in who she was.

Not him.

He was at ease. At one accord.

Finally, they arrived at the summit. Finally they arrived back at the house.

"Go and put something else on," he said.

She looked up at him, beseeching.

"Go," he said.

She emerged a few moments later wearing sweats.

"Now," he said. "You will sleep in my bed tonight."

"I will do no such thing."

"You have proven yourself to be a flight risk," he said. "And now I have to keep an eye on you. If you do not like the consequences… You have no one to blame but yourself. And I mean that for every piece of this, all the way down." He went into the bathroom and changed into a pair of athletic pants, only out of deference to the fact that he would be getting into bed with her. He was not normally so kind, but he also had no interest in terrorizing a woman in that regard.

Even if the woman in question was a holy terror herself.

She was standing there in his bedroom with a mutinous expression on her face. He ignored her, and wrapped his arm around her waist, picking her up and bringing her down into the bed with him. "As jail cells go, you must admit this is a warm one."

"But it's still a jail cell," she whispered.

"Forgive me if I do not find myself to be overly concerned with your protestations. You should've thought of that before any of this."

They lay there in darkness, her softness nestled against him, and desire bloomed in his midsection. This was an exercise in restraint, and he was not a man who normally put himself in the situations that required any.

He should hate her, this woman, for she had upended his well-ordered life.

He had not planned on taking a wife, least of all her. Especially not after what she had done.

And yet, he desired her. And there was nothing to be done about that. It simply was.

It simply was.

And in the morning, there was a phone call, telling him definitively that the child was his. And he knew that their path was now set in stone. There was no turning back now.

CHAPTER TWELVE

SHE WAS IN a dreamless sleep, cocooned in warmth. And when she woke up, the sun was shining bright in the room. She couldn't make heads or tails out of where she was, not for a moment. And then, suddenly, she remembered.

She was in Gunnar's room, and Gunnar's house. Because she had tried to run away last night, and she had nearly frozen to death and then he had dragged her naked into a hot springs. And that was now too many times that she had been unconscious in the presence of that man.

She was starting to feel like what she had never been. A wilting flower, incapable of standing on her own feet. That wasn't her. It never could be.

It wasn't her.

She was supposed to be better than that. She was supposed to be stronger. It was important that she...

She could hear herself, talking, what she had told him last night. It was the saddest admission she could think of. The way that she had said that she was basically a shadow person. The way that she seemed to think that it was acceptable.

She had never articulated those things before, and she wasn't sure why she had done it now. Hypothermia. It had to be. Because it just didn't make sense otherwise.

It was just…

It was just all a little bit too much. These last few days that she had spent in Gunnar's house were the only real vacation she'd had in years. And this was basically a kidnap. And it felt like a vacation.

She rolled over onto her back. And that was when she remembered he had slept holding her in his arms all night. But he was up now.

She flushed, thinking about it.

How could she not? She still wasn't used to all that kind of thing. She flushed even more thinking about the hot springs. About the way his hard, hot body had felt pressed up against hers.

Really, if she could be aroused thinking about a situation wherein she was maybe dying, it was really very bad.

She got out of bed, and padded out to the living area. And he was standing there, arms crossed over his broad chest. He was wearing a black sweater, and black pants, and the outfit looked like it could barely contain his muscles. But she could not ignore the fact that it was an outfit that looked alarmingly like the one that she typically liked to wear every day. The one that he had denied her.

She opened her mouth to say something, but the forbidding nature of his expression stopped her.

"What?"

"The paternity test results are back. I am the father."

"Well. I knew that already, Gunnar. I think you did too."

He said nothing.

"But you said to me that…that love is hard for you and I just don't understand…" She cleared her throat. "Why are you so intent on having me? On having the baby?"

He said nothing for a moment, his eyes going so cold they made the snow outside look like it might be a retreat into summer. "Do you know, I went to live with my father when I was twelve years old."

She shook her head. "I didn't know that. I just assumed that…"

"Of course you would assume I had always been with him. But no. Until I was twelve I was raised by my maternal grandparents. When I was older, when I wasn't a little boy, I thought I wanted to go and live with my father, you see. He sent me letters. From time to time. And I idolized him. I looked up photos of him on the Internet. I thought that he was brilliant. Exactly the sort of man I wanted to be when I grew up. I wanted to meet him more than anything in the world. I wanted to live with him. And when I was twelve I got my wish."

"Gunnar…"

"I still remember the thrill of it. He came in a helicopter. He was wearing a suit. He looked exactly like he had in the photos. And I knew… I knew that it was the right thing. He took me to where he was living in

London. I had never seen a city. It was… It was incredible.

"It did not take long for me to realize that he was not the man that I had dreamed him to be. There were women. Always in the home. In various states of undress. They were… They were paid to be there. Or perhaps manipulated. I came to find out later that he had a close association with a rather infamous man who was renowned for trafficking women. I will always wonder if those women were there of their own accord or not."

"That's terrible."

"It is. Of course, I was a boy, and I did not know the meaning of those women wandering about in flimsy robes. But I could see the way that he treated them. The disdain. As if they were something beneath him." He took a breath. "I understand now, that this was his cruelest abuse. But when I was a boy I only knew the pain of what he did to me. He kept my room Spartan and spare. And that, I did have feelings about. Because I missed my toys, no matter how humble they had been. I missed… But he said that I could not have toys. He said that I could not have friends."

And at sixteen, he'd eaten her birthday cupcake, and she'd thought him a villain. When he was a boy with a room that had nothing nice, and probably had no sweets, judging by the collection of candy he kept in that room.

The cupcake meant something else now.

Something different than it had before.

"That's awful."

"Is it so different from you? Is it so different from what your father did to you?"

"My father taught me to be hard. He taught me to win at all costs. But I had toys. He… He did treat me with some affection. It was not entirely void of those things."

"My father thought that beatings would teach me to be hard."

"Gunnar…"

"You see, Olive, I was as wrong about my father as I could've been about anyone. There was no way I could possibly have misjudged him more. We fell out finally when I was eighteen. There was a woman staying in the house, she could not have been much older than I. My father raised a hand to her. I would have none of it. I beat the hell out of him. And I regret nothing. I called the police, but she was unwilling to speak to them. I tried to help her, tried to get her to leave whatever situation she was in, but she… She was afraid. She ran before I could get her name, and I… I regret that bitterly. I have endeavored to do better than him because I have seen the destruction that a man with unchecked power can have on the world. I've seen the scars. I bear them."

Her throat was tight, with anger, sadness, all for him. But also…fear. For her child. For her future. "Let me ask you, truly. Why is it that you want to be a father to this child?"

"To protect them. It seems absurd, and yet… If they have you, and they have me… There is accountability."

"You won't let me hurt them, and I won't let you?"

"Yes. There is the possibility of course the both of us could be toxic."

"We won't be. We can make a different choice. For the baby. For us. We can make better choices."

"No child of mine will grow up without his father. And when I say that…"

"Why not? What do you care?"

"I'm not leaving it up to you," he said.

"That's offensive," she said.

"No. I will have my child, and I will have you. He will have a family that is together. That is married. I will not have…"

"Why?" She raised her hands in exasperation. "Neither of us had mothers, Gunnar. Neither of us had nuclear families. I am willing to give up Ambient. I'm willing to give it up." Her voice fractured, as she realized how true all of this was. "Because I can't have a child raised in boardrooms. Because I can't have a child be raised simply to be an afterthought. Simply to be an instrument for which to continue to carry out our bidding. It needs to be something else. We need to be something else."

"Then you may do that. If you choose. No one is forcing you to continue on as head of Ambient. But we will do this together."

"Well, make me understand what you're thinking then, because I'm the person that's having your baby, after all, and I think I ought to know what you're thinking. I think I ought to know why I have to be subject to your whim simply because you…" But the expression on his face stopped her short. There was something raw there, something ragged. Even in his anger at her he had managed to affect a sort of smoothness. An *I'm not mad I'm disappointed kind of countenance,* even though she had a feeling he was volcanic.

But this was different. This was a locked door. There was more to what had happened with his father, and he wasn't sharing it.

"What happened to you?" she asked.

"It does no good to speak of. All you need to know is what you are expected to do. I expect that you will give me what I ask for. I expect that you will marry me. Because if you do not, it is not only the company I will take."

"Gunnar..."

"Then what will you suggest, if we don't marry? Will I take the child for six months, and you another six? Will you surrender him to me completely? How do you suppose we make this work, if not the way I've commanded."

"I'm going to carry this child. I'm going to feel it move. I'm going to... How I feel now has nothing to do with how I'll feel in a few months, and already I... When I think of the baby, I can't help but..." She felt so raw and fragile, like she was cracking apart. In her desperation she had offered up the thing that mattered most to her. The thing that she defined herself by. Mostly because she was desperate to make sure that she did not raise a child in a world where that was all that mattered. When it was the only way that they mattered. Because it just felt... Wrong. It felt wrong, and she couldn't do it.

She didn't know what that would make her. The idea of not having Ambient made her feel rootless. Adrift.

But the idea of raising a child who would feel like she did about their life, about the world, that did not seem acceptable.

Her life hadn't been happy.

She'd tried to be happy in it. She'd tried her best but there had been no softness. No real…affection. Her father had set a hurdle and she'd done her best to clear it. Then there would be another, and another and she had learned to equate the praise she got for jumping over them with…love.

And she knew he had loved her. But it had been conditional.

She'd been happy to idolize her father's memory until she'd had to think about what sort of parent she wanted to be, and that had started to erode everything.

Because she would not do this to her child.

The last eight months had been hell. What she'd gone through, what she'd stooped to to try and make her father proud…

She didn't know herself.

And as she stood there she realized that was one of her problems.

She didn't know herself.

"What I said to you last night," she said. "That was honest. I don't know who I am apart from this corporation. I don't know who I am if I'm not succeeding. If I'm not chipping away at my own comfort in order to make things happen. It's the only thing I believe in. And I want a new god, quite frankly. Because this one hasn't served me very well. It's given me money. It's given me…" She shook her head. "All I ever wanted was to make him proud. All I ever wanted was to make it so that he didn't resent the fact that he had to drag me to all those board meetings and…"

"They could've hired nannies. They were billionaires. What your father chose to do with you during the day, had nothing to do with you. Not really. That was what he was doing to try to cultivate you into what he wanted. He could've had you back at home, couldn't he? He could have made sure that you were safe and comfortable, in a playroom with lots of toys. You do not have to be there on your birthday. You could've been home with balloons and a pony ride, hell, he could have changed the day of the meeting. Because he is not a nine-to-five worker drone, he owned the company."

He was rubbing salt in her wounds and while this was certainly the moment for honesty, this hurt, and she wanted to hit back at him.

"And if he would've showed that kind of weakness what do you think your father would've done?"

"He would've exploited it. He would've exploited the hell out of it, because you may have noticed that I was not home with nannies either. Nor was I receiving birthday parties of any kind. But still. These were choices that they made. To shape us into a very particular thing. You have nothing to make up to your father for. Nor do I."

The realization rocked her, because he wasn't wrong. He was… He spoke the truth. Her father didn't have to bring her to those meetings. She had this idea, this narrative that she had built in her mind of the single dad who had done his very best and dragged her along because he wanted to spend time with her. But they didn't spend time together. And it was thoroughly manipulative. They did not spend time together, and what he had been doing was showing her what she needed to value most. What he had been doing was teaching her that there was no such thing as a personal life.

He had been teaching her to erase boundaries. To not respect her need for a break. Leading by example, sure, but his dream didn't have to be her dream.

Now, standing there in this living room, as far as all of it had taken her, she wasn't sure what her dream was.

She was twenty-six years old, and the lone female CEO of any of the tech companies. The youngest too.

She didn't know if she wanted it. And it wasn't simply that cliché of knowing she was going to have a baby, but it had certainly done something to shake up her priorities.

As had passing out two different times in front of Gunnar. Maybe she was weak because she didn't have any stores built up. Maybe strength wasn't about how hard you could push yourself, but the restraint that you could show sometimes too.

Maybe there was a strength in saying no. One that she had certainly never found.

"I'll marry you," she said. "On one condition."

She saw it clearly now. She needed to get off the path her father had put her on.

She needed her own path.

The one that would lead her to herself. To Olive. The best person she could be, the best mother she could be.

"And what is that?"

"I want you to invest in a start-up."

"What will your start-up be?"

"I don't know. And maybe it won't end up being a start-up per se. I have no idea. Not yet. But I want you to invest in me, and what I decide I want. It won't be until a year after the baby is born, and by then I should have some ideas. I will marry you, as long as I can still figure out who I am. Because all of this is making me realize that I actually don't know. I don't feel guilty about the corporate espionage, not really. Because I know why I did it. What makes me feel strange is the fact that you know that's a hard limit for you, and I don't know what is for me. I don't know myself. I'm a hollowed-out vessel that my dad created to carry out his dreams, his ambitions. His wishes. And I don't want to be that. Not anymore. Because if I do, then I'll do the same to my child. I will carve them out and make them into something less than a person. Something less than a whole human being. And I cannot have that. I won't. It's not right or fair."

"That's a pretty speech. And if you wish, of course I will do that."

"And what will you expect. From a wife. Out of… Having a child."

"I offer protection. I offer fidelity."

Heat swept over her body, because of course. Of course to be married to him would be to sleep with him. But the idea filled her with a kind of reckless heat that she hadn't anticipated.

"What about…" Her throat suddenly felt scratchy. "Love? Not for me, obviously. Obviously not me. But the baby. Our baby."

"I offer protection. That as far as I'm concerned is an expression of something that many people might call love."

She looked at him, at that icy façade. "You don't believe in love, do you?"

"Oh, I believe in it. Many people around me have experienced it. Who am I to deny them what they feel. I just am no longer capable of it myself."

"You said that already but I don't…"

"Olive, I let you negotiate because there is no point in the two of us being miserable. But you do not get to set the terms here."

"This isn't a business negotiation, actually, Gunnar. For the first time, we are not talking about the terms of a business deal. Were talking about a human child. Our child."

"In our experience, that is much the same thing."

"No. It doesn't matter what our experience was. It doesn't matter… We cannot do things this way."

"Our child will have two parents. That is a beginning."

But it wasn't a promise of anything fantastic or romantic. Not at all. He condemned their childhood but without love…

Without love how would their child's life be different?

How would her life be different?

He was cold, and he was remote. He was the very frozen wasteland outside.

You'll have to do it. You'll have to create enough love to cover you and the baby.

"I'm going to be putting out an announcement about our upcoming marriage."

And suddenly, she realized what that would mean.

The world was going to explode. They were the most storied business rivals in modern history, and they were getting married. Having a baby. For all the world to see, merging their companies. Beneath the umbrella of his.

It was a decisive victory for Magnum. At least, that was how it would look to everyone else.

And she decided then, that she had to let it go. That she could no longer live to serve a public performance. Because she had to worry about whether or not something was a victory for *her life*. For the child.

Nothing else could matter, nothing else could be more important.

And that meant letting go. Stripping away the things that she used to mark success. "Well then," she said. "I imagine when we go back to the real world there will be quite a show waiting for us."

"Undoubtedly. I hope you're ready."

She looked at him, her greatest boardroom rival, and now her fiancé. The father of her child. "I'm ready if you are."

He smiled, that wolfish smile. And this time she

realized that when he did so, it did not go all the way up to those steely blue eyes.

There was a reason he was like this, she knew it. And she had seen glimpses of a different man. A warmer man.

But he did his best to cover it.

And she had a feeling that she would never be powerful enough to melt all that ice.

CHAPTER THIRTEEN

"I LOOK LIKE a Russian trophy wife," Olive said as she settled back into the leather armchair on the plane, one booted foot stuck out in front of her. She was wearing spiked heels in a camel color, and a long white jacket, with a furry white hat perched atop her head.

He thought she looked soft, and far more delicious than any woman had a right to. But he could also see Russian trophy wife.

"Well. As of next week you will be my trophy wife."

"The idea of being your trophy sticks in a particularly…" She made a stabbing motion with her hand. "Rough place."

"To the victor go the spoils. In this case, I suppose the public notoriety."

"Well, we're going to be notorious, all right. Have you checked all of the socials?"

"Hell no," he said, waving a hand. "I have management teams for that kind of thing, I don't concern myself with the inanity of Internet chatter."

"Oh, you should," she said. "Sometimes it's hilarious. Honestly. Some people think that we are part of the evil one percent, conspiring to take over the world with this present merger. The wedding is obviously fake. We are aliens. We don't marry."

"I admit, that is a slightly more interesting take than what I expected."

"There's more."

"I told you I don't read these kinds of things."

"But I do. Welcome to marriage."

She grabbed her phone and sat up, scrolling through something. He didn't know what. "OMG, it's like a rom-com. Enemies to lovers."

"What the hell does that mean?"

"Oh, I don't know. But somebody said it on a social media site, therefore it's news." She continued to read. "For sure she is getting the better end of the deal. I hear that his broadsword is the size of—"

"What is this garbage?"

There was something about this that worked its way deeply beneath his skin. No one knew him. He didn't allow it. And all these people were talking about him as if they could.

If he would ever have allowed anyone to know him, it might have been Olive.

"I believe broadsword is a euphemism for your—"

"I am aware of what it is a euphemism for. What I don't understand is why. Why do people concern themselves with these things. They could be living their own lives, rather than chatting about the lives of others."

His life was not a spectator sport. Not a game. It had been marked by abuse and an extreme need to fix that which his father had done to scar the world.

He was marrying Olive to right yet more wrongs, and it was sharp and filled with danger. And these people called it a rom-com.

"People chat. They like to do it. It makes them feel connected. See, this is the thing that you missed. You make technology, but you failed to see the ways in which it can make beautiful things. You like to make functional things."

"People discussing a stranger's penis is hardly beautiful."

She scooted to the edge of her seat and doubled over, her furry hat falling into her face as she laughed. "Okay. Maybe beautiful is a stretch on this score. This is a shallow way that people use the Internet, but it's fairly harmless."

"Is it harmless? They talk about us as if they know us. They don't."

"Well, they feel like they do. And it has little reflection on our actual lives, it certainly doesn't impact us. But people connect. I think it's kind of beautiful. Something that could be cold, something that could be difficult… People have found a way to make it something different."

"Except when they decide to use it to burn down the lives of others. To hunt them down mercilessly and bring up a comment made ten years ago, and determine they're not allowed to have jobs or friends or… Even live."

"Granted," she said. "It has a dark side. Everything does. Because people do. Fundamentally, however we are expressing it, we are who we are. Isn't that the case?"

He grunted, and leaned back in his chair.

"I'm serious. Think about it. What is a public Internet shaming if not the stocks and pillories? And ostracizing of somebody for violating the way the group perceives morality. It's what we've always done. Computers don't change that. I mean, that's the thing. I understand why you think something like this is silly, or even harmful, but I just think it's human nature. We bring it with us wherever we go. And we bring it into modern technology."

"You're much more fascinated by the intricacies of human behavior than I am. I make products, and if they are useful, people will buy them. That is all. I don't need to understand the concept of public shaming to know that."

And yet he had to wonder if he was so averse to it because it felt…foreign to him in some ways. Unknowable.

"Really? I would've thought that you would find it interesting. We're always looking for the barbarian at the gate. Even if we have to make one up. And most especially, I think we have to make one up in this modern world."

"I thought you said you didn't have any friends. You sound like a person who is interested enough in the way that people behave and communicate that you want to."

She scrunched her nose. "I observe people. And this is what I think about them. I don't know. You don't like people, do you?"

"I don't like or dislike people until I get to know one of them. You speak of humanity. I don't care."

"Why not? I would've thought that somebody who was so invested in green energy would have a lot of thoughts on human nature."

"What does that have to do with human nature?"

"For example," she said. "You're never going to get people to switch to a green energy product unless it is convenient, less expensive, or remarkably better. People are all about their own convenience. And they might philosophically care about broader things, but at the end of the day, you have to make things appealing to them. Because most people have to get what they can afford. Or what feels nice if they have money. Or what is convenient, because God knows everybody is strapped for time, and the point of technological innovation is supposed to be convenience."

"An interesting perspective," he said. And he had to admit that it was. He tended to think of things in terms of right and wrong. To him, changing things to benefit the planet was right. And he felt that comfort, convenience... None of it could possibly be more important than that one moral truth.

Obviously, Olive saw things differently.

He thought again of the corporate espionage, and the way she had justified it.

"So what then does you stealing information from me fall under? Convenience? Luxury?"

"That was about loving someone," she said softly. She met his eyes. "I loved my father so much that there was nothing quite so important as making sure that he got what he wanted. Even if he wasn't here to see it. The more emotions get tangled up in situations like these, the less black and white they are. Because it shifts what's acceptable. And what isn't. For me, acceptable is only getting the contract my father wanted. And that's… It's changing. Inside of me. All the time. As things… As they change. As I think about what kind of mother I want to be." She looked up at him, her gaze dewy. "I had a realization, or, it skimmed past me yesterday, and just now it's beginning to bloom into a full-on epiphany. My father loved his company more than he ever loved me. For me, it was about loving him. As much as Ambient has been the biggest work of my life, my motivation in making it so was to make him proud. Because his investment in my childhood was entirely related to Ambient. Because what he considered a success was entirely related to Ambient. I wanted to make him proud. But he never wanted to be proud of me half so much as he wanted me to accomplish specific things. What he wanted was the result. Not the feeling. I think he wouldn't have cared at the end of the day if it were me or somebody else who had accomplished all these things, except that if it's me, it links more directly back to him and his legacy. It's convenient for him. You understand?"

"I suppose."

"The point is, that's what got me started on letting go of this. Because that isn't why I was doing this. You're doing things for achievements, that's why the cheating seems important to you. You want to know that you're the best. I just want to know that I did what my father asked of me. That's all. I also realize that I don't want to consign any child of mine to the same sort of fate. To this desperate need to make their dad proud. To this desperate need to perform to please a parent. Because it's… It's nearly impossible. It's such a weight, such a burden. And I just can't… I just can't put them under that."

"I do not know why my father did the things he did. He was a man with more money than God. He could have lived well and been decent. I will never understand him. But I know why I wanted to take control of Magnum and turned it into something better than he ever did."

"Why?"

"To prove I'm better. To prove that he was wrong. To prove that he is nothing."

To prove I'm not the same.

"Revenge?"

"If I'd sought revenge, I would have done it while he was alive. I want more than revenge. I want to make a change. My takeover of Magnum is essentially what I'm doing to Ambient. It has become part of the thing that I made. Which is bigger. And is the way of the future. These things are simply… Assets."

"And you don't care about them."

"My father thought that to care about things was a weakness. I do not respect my father, but if there is one thing I never allowed myself to become…it's weak."

His one indulgence was the house in Iceland. A faint echo of better times. Simpler times.

"My father wanted there to be no softness in me.

And he got his wish. But the fact is, the hand that sharpens the sword must be very careful that the sword is not turned upon him."

"That seems very Viking of you."

"You seem to have a preoccupation with Vikings."

Her cheeks went red.

"Well, it's just… It's just… I like… I like medieval Viking romance novels."

"You mentioned this before. I cannot believe romance stories about Vikings exist."

"I find them to be diverting."

"Vikings specifically."

"Yes."

"But they were raiders. Pillagers. More often than not, they would simply take women captive rather than marry them. How exactly can that be a romance?"

He lifted a brow and regarded her closely. He did not know why her answer seemed suddenly important.

"Wow, Gunnar, I cannot imagine why the story of a woman who is forced into a life against her will and must find softness and pleasure in it, in spite of circumstances she will never be fully in control over, would appeal to me."

And he didn't say anything, because he had to sit with that comment.

It was a strange perspective.

One he certainly had never thought of. And who did she feel trapped by? Her father?

He supposed that at the moment she felt trapped by him.

But he could not let her go.

He would not.

They would be married next week, in a wedding that was certain to be the media spectacle of the decade.

And she would simply have to continue to live in her world of romance novels and whatever else she might need.

He was not a man who could make a different choice than this.

And he could only indulge her so far.

He looked at her, all of her softness.

And he ached.

Once had not been enough.

But soon enough, she would be his bride. And then… Then he would have her.

Raiders. Pillagers.

Was he any different?

He had not imagined that he was a Viking.

But in that moment, he felt as if he were.

The conqueror, quite eager to take the conquered.

Except he looked at the stubborn line of her jaw, and she glanced at him out of the corner of her eye.

No. Olive would never be conquered.

Instead, it would be a battle every day forever.

And he ignored the tightening of excitement in his gut at the thought of that.

CHAPTER FOURTEEN

BY THE TIME they landed in New York, it felt as if the entire Internet had exploded.

Rumors about their affair and how long it had been going on, about the wedding, and who would be on the guest list.

And she realized, she would have to put that together, and quickly, so that it all looked a bit more thought out than it was.

But they should have no issues getting a raft of celebrities to attend. It was exactly the sort of thing that they loved to be seen at. Something that made them look smart and tied into a world that had nothing to do with the entertainment industry.

And something that would make her and Gunnar look even more like the illuminati. Which kind of amused her.

She was looking forward to going back to her apartment, but they didn't go there. In fact, they didn't even go into the city. Instead, she found herself in the back of a limousine, on a winding road that led... She didn't know where.

It became clear, when a large home came into view. "You have a house?"

She hadn't known that he had a place other than his New York penthouse in the States.

"I bought a house," he said.

"You… You just bought this?"

"Yes. I thought that it would make a wonderful wedding present to you, and we could set up a nursery here. You must admit, right in the heart of downtown hardly feels the appropriate place to have a baby."

"As if you have any idea of what to do with the baby," she said.

"I didn't say that I did. However, I do feel that I can confidently say that this is a better place to raise a child."

"Well. Your cliffside home is definitely not the most child friendly. Can you imagine if a baby got outside there?"

"This is silly. In Iceland, we simply teach children…"

"Whatever. In America we put leashes on them. Anyway. You probably should've talked to me about buying a house that we're going to live in."

"Why? I wish for you to get used to exactly how this relationship is going to work."

"You think you're in charge?"

She looked at him, and she didn't feel… Trapped. She didn't even feel particularly angry. But she was… Still puzzling over the things that she had figured out about him over the last little bit. The way that he talked about emotion. The way that he talked about his father.

That he had actually hated his father. She wanted to know what happened. She wanted to understand.

She really didn't know anything about his life. She felt like she did, because she saw him in a certain setting over a number of years, but a great amount of that was witnessed with a child's understanding of things, and the rest… It was just so specific to the situation they had been in.

And she had filled in a whole lot of details about him using her own life as a guide, and that was not necessarily the most honest way to do it.

She had been certain that she knew Gunnar, and now she realized that she really didn't.

"But you need to be in charge of this," she said. "Because it needs to be a decisive victory for you? Because this is how you prove you're better than me?"

"You make me sound like a petty child. As I said, I did not need to prove that I was better than you, I would simply not be able to rest knowing that I had not been the best, if that was my goal. I was happy always when you had the better product and won. It was fair. But if we are to have harmony in our home, then certain things must be understood. Certain things must be clear. That is the making of a good company, is it not?"

"But families aren't companies," she said. "And when you marry me, Gunnar, you are going to be my family."

He looked over at her, his blue eyes sharp. "I do not think that is a very fair characterization."

"It's just true. We are going to be a family. And

I think we need to… We need to not look at it like a business."

The car pulled up to the front of the house, and Gunnar got out, rounding to her side of the vehicle and opening the door for her.

She looked up at the place, a feat of modern crafts-manship, not wholly dissimilar to the house in Iceland, though formed instead around the landscape here. She opened the door, and turned circles as she looked at the palatial entry. There was a large chandelier in the doorway, that seemed to be made entirely of tubes of glass with little sparkling drops of air illuminated in-side of them.

"Wow," she said.

"Like my house in Iceland, all of it runs on green energy."

"See. You really do have the luxury part of it down. It's absolutely beautiful. And nobody could complain about not being comfortable here. That's for sure."

"Well, I'm glad you find it to your liking."

"I suppose I need to find something to my liking."

She wondered then if he wanted her. At all. Or if being married to her was going to feel like a life sen-tence.

She wondered if…

She wondered what he felt at all.

They had been fighting. And through all of it, she had not lost her desire for him. When he had taken her into the hot springs and held her close, in spite of the chill, she had felt rising desire for him. It had been…

It still made her hot just thinking about it.

She flushed even now, looking at him in the entry-way, and felt so ashamed that she had to turn away.

"Your room is up the stairs and down at the very end of the hall."

"Are we to have separate bedrooms?"

He looked at her, his eyes molten. "Of course. I should not like to take your space from you."

Or maybe he just didn't want her. And what did she want? She wanted him, but…

He was such a complicated man. And what she knew about complicated was it was only worse when there were feelings involved. Her feelings. The feelings he claimed he didn't have. Yes. There were a whole lot of feelings here, and she had a feeling that he would deny it, but it was the truth of it.

Having her own space would probably be a necessity.

For her sanity.

"Has anyone ever told you that you're infuriating?"

"A time or ten."

"What do you want, Gunnar? What do you want from me? Do you want simply to be husband and wife and bump around this giant house together? Do you want… Do you want me? I don't understand. You seem to want to turn me into something else. And as much as I kind of love this outfit, you know it's not what I prefer to wear. Are you throwing me in these things to change me, or is it simply to get at me? This is the thing, you know me. I think you might know me better than anyone else on earth. I thought I knew you. I'm trying to know you. But I wonder if I do, even a little. Even at all."

He moved toward her then, fire in his eyes. He backed her up against the wall there in the entry. And there it was. Her Viking marauder.

It made her heart throb with desire. Made that place between her legs ache.

Yes, her soul whispered. *Take me.*

Because that would make sense. It would make sense because she wanted him. Because it was how they had gotten here. Because of the desire between them, and the two of them denying it for these past few days while all of these intense changes happened around them… It made her feel disconnected from it all. But this reminded her.

It reminded her that in a sea of uncertainty, there was this. There was him.

"You do not wish to be strangers in the house together? I should've thought that that would be to your liking. I should've thought that it would make things easier."

"Nothing makes this easier. But at least…" She didn't know if she wanted to shame herself like this. "At least if there's this…" She reached out and put her hand on his chest, and she found herself being pulled toward him.

"This is just sex."

It wasn't, though.

Because if it was only sex, it would have eased by

now. Or faded slightly, but there was none of that. Instead, it came alive with an intensity that threatened to destroy everything else. Threatened to destroy all that they were. Threatened to burn her where she stood. She wanted him. She wanted to burn in this. To burn in him. She wanted desperately to get out of her head. She wanted to fracture this thing between them. To make it as undeniable for him as it was for her.

She wanted to get through that hard layer of ice in his chest. He was in control. That was what bothered her. That he was maddeningly endlessly in control.

Everything seemed logical to him. If the baby was his, then they would get married. If not, he would send her to prison. And none of it spoke to any kind of feeling for her or for the child or anything. None of it spoke to the spark between them. None of it seemed to matter to him. And it felt astronomically and categorically unfair. That he could remain so untouched by all of this when she was upended. When she was ready to give up the pursuit of her life. The company, when she was reevaluating her entire relationship with her father. Her relationship with herself. Her relationship with everything.

But in this, she felt as if they were equalized. In this, she could feel her own power.

He wanted her. She could see that even now, even as he stood, poised as if on a knife's edge, unmoving. Like a predator. Lying in wait. Even in that, she could see how difficult it was for him to seize control. And she gloried in that. Because it made her feel like perhaps she wasn't the only one. It made her feel as if she wasn't alone.

She desperately didn't want to be alone.

But she waited. Waited for him to break. Because she needed him to. Waited for him to break, because it was the assurance that she needed. Because she needed control. She needed power. Even while she needed for him to claim her. To brand her.

It didn't matter if that made sense to anyone else, it made sense to her. She wanted. With hot reckless greed. With a deep abandon that she hadn't experienced in any other part of her life.

What she wanted for Ambient, she wanted on behalf of her father. What she wanted was to please him. And everything she did she had done with precision. But what she did, what she wanted, with Gunnar had nothing to do with precision. It had nothing to do with logic and everything to do with need. And she wanted to become that. Wanted to embrace it. She wanted to become his, and through that, become more of herself.

And maybe no one else could ever understand that, maybe if it were someone else, it wouldn't make any sense. But they were them. And even feeling like she did, even feeling like she didn't know him to the degree that she wished, to the degree that she had imagined, she knew that they were something that no one else was. The media could make proclamations about them all they wanted. The world could post about how they were this and that and something else entirely, but they weren't anything except for Gunnar and Olive. And they couldn't be. Not ever.

Nobody would ever be them. And no one would ever be him for her. He was everything. Everything and glory, and he made her want to be more. Somehow, even with all that iciness in his soul, he made her want to find her warmth. Or maybe that was why. Because she wanted so much to do something for him. To fix him.

Or maybe not even that. Just knowing him… That would be enough. That would be enough. She wondered if anyone did. And she imagined they didn't. That he kept himself as closed off as possible. The human representation of that house of his, up on the hill.

And he was the one this time who gave in. The one who growled, lowering his head to hers and claiming her lips in a searing vow.

Whatever they would say to each other in that church, this week, whatever promises they would make in front of the world, they didn't matter. Not compared to this. To this moment, with this man. He was everything, and they were incendiary. The rest of this, it would be a performance. The union for their child. But this? This was all them. Only them. A lack of control, a flaw in their personal systems. But it could not be denied, nor could it be controlled. He gripped her face, shoving his fingers through her hair, pushing the fur hat off of her head and onto the floor. She had chosen the outfit to be deliberately ridiculous. Soft when she normally went for severe. But she had to admit she sort of loved the hat. And the boots. And the coat. But all she wanted was to get all of it off now. She wanted there to be nothing between them. No barriers. Nothing. She wanted to give herself over to him entirely. To surrender to this, him.

And he kissed her. And kissed her, as if there was no particular hurry, and a ticking clock all at once.

He kissed her, his tongue sliding against hers, his big rough hands moving over her body.

She loved the feel of him. She loved everything about him. And the real problem was, she had always loved Gunnar more than she had ever loved her company. And that realization nearly made her knees buckle. But it was true.

He fascinated her, bewitched her, beguiled her, and had shaped her every fantasy from the first moment she had begun to have them. And it wasn't simply because there had been no one else around. She could see no one else because of Gunnar. He blinded her to everything and everyone that wasn't him. He was essentially everything. And it was not a lack of opportunity, a lack of skills, a lack of beauty, that had kept her away from other men.

It was the all-consuming desire for this one man. And not simply desire. She had felt when she was a girl that she understood him. And she knew now as a woman that she did not. But whatever was behind the ice blockade, she wanted him.

And perhaps that was the real truth of it. The real deep certainty of love.

That if she kept going, if she went deeper. She would still care. That she would accept him. That he could reveal to her any sort of new truth about him and she would simply kiss him and be grateful that he trusted her enough to tell her.

He was the spark to her flame, and she knew that, and it was enough. The man who could keep up with her. Who could challenge her. She respected his mind, his drive.

He was her equal. But even better than that, he was a mystery as well. And that was fascinating, more than anything ever had been.

The way he was known and unknown. The way he was like her and yet so different all at once.

And it was more than just their physical differences, but it was highlighted even now. He was so large. So hard.

And she began to greedily strip away the layers of his clothing as he kissed her, as he licked into her mouth.

She undid the buttons on his shirt, pushed it and his jacket down onto the floor. She gloried in the broad expanse of his chest, the hair there, the sculpted muscle.

She moved her fingertips down to skim his abdominal muscles, and she whimpered.

She wanted him more now than she had the first time, because now she knew how good it felt. She had explained away how aroused she had been that first time they were together with the simple explanation that it was years of pent-up longing. But now it wasn't that.

It was simply their chemistry that threatened to consume her. And she wanted it to. She was more than happy to drown in it.

He gripped her chin, and her hair, forcing her head back and taking the kiss impossibly deep. She moaned, writhing up against his body.

He picked her up from where they stood and carried her from the entryway, into a living area where there was a plush, wide couch.

It did not look as if it was especially made for sitting, but rather it was made for something like this. Black and round, with ample space for how athletic she knew the sex was between them.

She had never really considered herself an athlete. But he made her want to endeavor to be one.

At least, he made her happy enough to exert herself where typically she found that sort of thing overrated. There was nothing overrated about this.

She could honestly say, that for all the big deal people made out of sex… She could see why. Ten out of ten. Would recommend.

And then she couldn't think anymore, because Gunnar was methodically stripping her clothes from her body, licking his way across all of her skin. Teasing her, tormenting her.

He turned her over onto her knees, and wrapped his arm around her waist, lifting her up. Then she heard the sound of his belt buckle coming undone, and she came undone along with it.

She felt the blunt head of his arousal pressed against the entrance to her body, and she moaned. He slid into her slowly from behind, the new position making things unbearably tight. Making her feel so full.

The raw sound that came from her lips was animal. Foreign.

She loved it. She loved what he did to her. The way that he took her every expectation about herself and turned it inside out. The way that he changed her into something new.

And he had. That was the most extraordinary realization of all. The woman that had agreed to marry him, the woman that had decided to try something different. To try being someone different, to try and make a life that wasn't in service to a dead man who had never loved her more than a corporation, that woman had been forged in the fires of passion with Gunnar. And yes, much of the heat and strength came from inside of her, it took two of them to create this alchemy after all.

He gripped her hips, a short curse on his lips as he began to thrust hard into her body.

She loved this. This animalistic passion that created in them something entirely new.

"Gunnar," she moaned his name, and he growled.

"Olive," he said.

And she knew that he was with her. She knew that he was as much enslaved by this as she was.

How she loved him.

And it made her cry out. Because it was a terrible thing to love him. A horrible thing. And yet it was the inevitable thing. It was fate. She couldn't deny it.

He had always, and only ever, been the one man for her.

This moment had been written for her long before she had ever picked up a romance novel.

Except the problem was, she wasn't sure she would get her happy ending. Oh, he would marry her. He was a man of integrity. He would keep his word. She knew that. And that was what scared her. He didn't love her. He didn't love her. And what was she supposed to do with the knowledge that he would not. Could not. Did she persevere. She had no choice. She knew that. She had no choice, because... Whatever was behind the wall. She wanted him.

The question was, would she ever be able to get behind it.

"Gunnar," she moaned when the large head of him scraped up against something sensitive and glorious inside of her. And she began to tremble. Began to shake.

She wasn't going to be able to hold out for much longer, her desire overwhelming her. A thunderstorm of need. He gripped her hips hard, and she hoped—she desperately hoped—that he would leave bruises behind. She wanted to be able to look at herself and see that she was as physically changed as she was emotionally.

This man.

She felt as if he had grabbed a loose thread of hers once long ago, and had been pulling it ever since, and now she was threadbare, worn, and desperately trying to cover herself up. And yet, it was the beauty of it. The utter beauty. Her brokenness. The places where she could no longer hide.

It allowed her to see herself for the first time.

And yes, it left her open to him as well. And she felt bright and scalded and new, shaking as she was, while he destroyed the version of all it that had existed before.

She lowered her head to the velvet couch and pressed her face into it, balling her hands into fists and shuddering out her pleasure, while he suddenly growled out his own.

"Yes," she whispered. She wanted it all. Everything. Everything he could ever be.

Everything they could ever be.

And when it was done, he pulled away from her, and he began straightening himself, as if it hadn't just dissolved the two of them.

"It is good that there is attraction between us," he said, his tone sounding remote.

And she felt devastated. Because it was more than attraction. It was more than chemistry. It changed her.

"Maybe we won't need separate rooms."

"I imagine it will be good for you to have your space," he said.

And what she heard, inarguably and unequivocally, was that he wanted his own space. Away from her.

And that was fine. It was. She had to accept him. And if she couldn't do that then…

Tears filled her eyes, but she turned herself away quickly to avoid allowing him to see.

"Our things have been moved in already."

"You really are efficient," she said.

"There's no point doing anything if it's not done efficiently."

"Even screwing your fiancée, I guess."

He lifted a brow. "Have you a complaint?"

"I'm not complaining. It felt wonderful."

"But?"

"Nothing."

And she would not speak to him about the fact that he clearly didn't want to show her any tenderness, or get to know her anymore than he already did. She would say nothing about the fact that she had experienced something transformative just now, and he looked as he ever did.

She would not say that she loved him. Because she had a feeling that it would be the most cardinal sin, and yet if he really felt nothing, why would it matter? She just knew that it did. She knew that it would. She knew that he would take that and reject it so violently it would leave it torn and bloodied, and it was too new for her to take a chance on that.

So she said nothing. So she kept it all in her own heart. Kept it all to herself.

Because what would be the point. Of any of it.

"I guess I'll go to my room then."

"Yes. That sounds a good idea. You are likely tired."

She really resented him telling her what she was. What she felt.

Especially in light of everything. That he had created the feelings in her, and she knew that he would do nothing to soothe them.

She went into the bedroom, and she had to laugh. Because this looked nothing like his home in Iceland.

This was completely different. This was… Her. And yes, she knew that a designer had done it, and quickly, but she imagined that he had asked them to take their inspiration from her existing apartment. To take it and find a new way to express it so that it felt like her, but also felt fresh.

Gunnar. Oh, Gunnar.

She slept fitfully, and the next morning she wandered around the massive house alone. She wasn't certain if Gunnar was even in residence.

She had a croissant and a tea for breakfast, then answered some work emails. After an hour or so she was restless.

The house was incredible. Huge. There were so many rooms, and any one of them could be the nursery. *The nursery.*

Her heart squeezed tight. She was here, committed to making a family with Gunnar. Committed to…

There was so much between them. Heat and anger and despair.

She wanted more.

She didn't know if he would ever give her more.

She started to push the doors open, looking inside. There was nothing remarkable about any of them. And there was one door, painted blue. She stopped, and pushed it open. And inside was… It was nearly identical to the room in Gunnar's home in Iceland, except there was a crib in it. But the walls were painted bright colors, and there were games, toys. She walked out of the hallway. "Gunnar?"

She heard footsteps coming up the stairs. "What is it?"

"Did you have a nursery put together for the child?"

He stopped at the top of the stairs and nodded gravely. "Yes."

"It looks like… The room in Iceland. Was that meant to be a nursery too? Except… It didn't have a crib in it… It's because your father took your toys."

"Olive…"

"It is. It's because your father took your toys, and you replaced them." Her chest went horribly tight. "Gunnar…" She moved to him, and she touched his face. "You're going to be a good father."

He turned his head away. "I choose to be a good man. I choose to do good things."

"You are a good man."

"Any man is capable of being corrupted."

"Is that an accusation directed at me?"

"I can see how you would think it might be given our history. But no. This is about me. And what I know of men. Men like my father."

"I've never seen you display a violent temper. Even when you were angry with me in my office… I fainted and you took me to the doctor."

"And yet it is complacency that could create problems. I will never be complacent."

But he had bought all these toys. It was like the only way he knew to show affection. And suddenly… She was filled with hope. Hope for their future. He had said that he could not love, but what was this if not... The very depths of his soul brought out before them. The one thing he had wanted more than anything. It was a physical representation of what he had thought a father's love might be, and what he had been denied. And here it was. Here it was.

"It's beautiful."

"It may not work for a girl," he said.

"It's perfect. It's perfect no matter what. We are not our fathers. Our child will have birthday parties here. In the yard, with friends. And there will be ponies."

"Ponies?"

"Yes. And chocolate cupcakes."

And she saw something soften in him.

"Perhaps."

"What else happened? With your father."

Gunnar shrugged. "He did not believe in spoiling me. Which to him meant not giving me any softness. He left me locked in my room for large swaths of time—primarily from the time I was twelve to fourteen, after that he began to take me to different events. If I didn't perform the way he wanted me to...there would be consequences."

"He hurt you," she said, her chest feeling like lead.

"Yes."

"But look at all this. Look at how you...you want to give different things to our child. That matters. It counts for something." She needed him to know that. He looked so bleak she just...needed him to know that.

"The past has shaped me into the man I am today,

and a room full of toys and good intentions doesn't... There is only so much I can offer."

He meant that. She could see that he did. But she just didn't understand why. She could see that he cared. She could see it in this room around her.

She could feel it in his touch.

"The past doesn't matter. It doesn't have to matter."

And then something shuttered in his expression. "I wish that were so. But as far as I'm concerned... One must learn from the past. Or there was never any point to it at all."

And then he walked away. From the moment, as he always did.

But the nursery remained. A real, beautiful testament to something, to more.

What he'd wanted as a child.

What he wanted to be as a father.

Why was he like this? Why was he so infuriating. So maddening, and yet so wonderful, all at once. Why was... It seemed like they had a connection. It just seemed also like he would want to deny it.

And everything in her ached for that to not be the case.

But she could not ignore the fact that he seemed remote. That he'd said he would never love.

Well. She was beginning to think she had never really been loved before.

Her father had affection for her. He had been kind to her—conditionally. But it wasn't the same. It certainly wasn't the same as what she wanted to give to her child.

She blinked, scrunching her eyes tight.

She would make it through this. And she would not give in to despair. She had this room, and it showed that he saw her. On some level, he saw her.

And in the dark of night when she slept in this bed alone, she would remember that, and the way he had held her in the hot springs, and she would use that to keep her warm and insulated against all the ice.

CHAPTER FIFTEEN

THE LEAD-UP TO the wedding was intense, but well handled. If there was one thing that he and Olive knew, it was how to delegate, and how to formulate a plan. The two of them together setting this into motion made it seem satisfyingly easy. Watching all of the pieces work in time with each other really was incredibly satisfying.

And he... He found that he liked the way that he and Olive worked together. They had been sparring against each other for so many years, that he had not been aware of the fact the two of them could create something so spectacular when they used their gifts in tandem.

But Olive was particularly brilliant at getting the best out of people. She excelled with team management and with aesthetics. She was a hard worker, and she knew how to adjust things to make them just that much more special. Just that much more pleasing to the eye.

He was good with mechanics. With the way things ran, and how they would work. He was good at organizing tasks.

They complemented each other in a way that he

could never have foreseen. He had not thought he'd had blind spots remaining in his life, and yet, this was a large one.

But he had never understood Olive and her quirkiness. The way that she behaved, or the way that she looked at things, but he could see now that it was an essential part of what she was. An essential part of who she was. Without it, she would not come up with things that she did.

Without it, she would not be Olive.

He had watched her march around the room eating saltine crackers, making suggestions to how the reception decor might be shifted slightly, that changed something from lovely to unbearably brilliant.

She was bright. And smart. She was a spark that he could not look away from.

And the day of the wedding, she made herself scarce, texting him about how it was bad luck for the groom to see the bride.

He also had not been with her again since that first day they had moved into the new house.

Their encounter on the sofa had been incendiary, and he had nearly been undone by it altogether.

The moment in the nursery had been something else entirely.

He could not quite understand, this thing that she did to him. He could not quite understand what it was she made him. For he was accustomed to having a sexual appetite, but he was not accustomed to being controlled by it. He was not accustomed to being at its mercy, but when she had stood there, looking up at him as she had, it had been outside of his power to resist. He had kissed her when they'd first arrived, because he'd had no other choice. He had kissed her, because he had been unable to stop himself. She was all things brilliant and beautiful, but it was more than that. He had had any number of beautiful women, and he could go out today and get more, even if they knew that his wedding was today. Maybe most especially if they knew.

But they would never be Olive, and they would never do to him what she did.

She fascinated him.

And if he were honest with himself, he could admit that she always had. It had been easy to write it off as some twisted form of forbidden lust, but that would take it and oversimplify it far too much. It was not that. No. It was something without a name. Something without measure. Something that made him think of a tiny home in the middle of nowhere in Iceland. Smoke coming out of the chimney, a simple meal of fish and bread.

A life where there had not been money, but there had been a warmth that he had not felt since.

And he had been cold. Every day of his life since he had left that cabin. Cold, except for when Olive ignited within him.

He had no one standing up with him at his wedding. And neither did Olive. It spoke volumes but neither of them had another person to ask to fulfill such a duty. They could have manufactured friends out of nothing, but they had both agreed that there was no need to be performative. Not when the rest of it was such a performance.

They were marrying outdoors at a massive estate, because Olive had said it would be atmospheric, and she wished to embrace that over tradition.

And he deferred to her, because she had been right about many things all along, so why not that.

The guests were all there, seated and looking appropriately like the sort of people that should be at a wedding that united two of the largest tech moguls in the entire world.

The performance was impeccable.

And as he stood there and waited for his bride, he felt the sense of performance begin to slip away.

His parents had never married. It was one reason he felt so strongly about this.

He had never known his mother.

But her parents… They had been warm and wonderful people.

They had been the only real taste of family he'd ever had.

And yet, he could not get back to that. He did not know how to find it. The loss of them was something that had frozen him over, and he had never yet found his way back. Not to himself. Not to anything else.

Nothing that felt half so much like home.

And then Olive appeared in his vision, walking across the grass, between the chairs. And he nearly laughed. She was not wearing black. But she was wearing a white wedding dress with long sleeves and an extremely high neck. It was elegant, and perfect, like the rest of her, but also inarguably shaped like her preferred black turtlenecks.

It was essentially her, to make that reference, perhaps one that only he would understand. And she would make it slyly all the same.

She was holding a large bouquet of flowers, all in fall colors, her brown hair down and curling, swept to the side over her shoulder.

She had never looked more beautiful.

It was enough to drive him to his knees. It was enough, to harken back to his raider ancestors, make him wish to pick her up and carry her out over his shoulders so he could make love to her, rather than stand here with her in front of an audience.

But the audience was necessary.

The rest of it was not.

When she arrived at the front, she had no bridesmaids to hand her bouquet to, so she turned to the crowd and cheerfully tossed it out. There was a minor celebrity in the third row who caught it and screamed excitedly.

Oh, yes. Olive was wonderful at a spectacle.

She knew how to command attention.

She always had.

Her tech presentations where she debuted the year's new technology for Ambient had been huge events for the last few years. Building in popularity each and every time.

She was just that way. Just undeniably that way.

He was not a man given to socializing. And the truth was, he had never been to a wedding. He never had occasion to. He had certainly never attended as anyone's date, and had never felt beholden enough to somebody to have to review the spectacle himself.

And so the words of the vows were unfamiliar to him, something foreign, even though he had seen abbreviated versions of them in movies. But not many. He didn't watch a lot of movies. Occasionally one would play in the background on the plane.

How could you promise such things to another person? And how can they promise them to you and expect to keep them in any kind of fashion? He found it a daunting thing to think of. And the divorce rate was so high. And yet humans did this. And expected theirs to last.

The unbearable optimism of some people amazed him.

He had lost his own when he'd been twelve years old.

He had traded his own. Sold it. For thirty pieces of silver, as it were.

Olive was saying her vows, bright and clear and true, her eyes shining, and anyone might've thought that she meant them.

It did something to him. To hear that.

To see her pledge her loyalty to him. Her… Her love. But then, he had just promised the same thing, and he had no concept of love.

Not really.

And when it was time to kiss, it was a relief. Because he understood that. The physicality between them was undeniable, and there was a familiarity to it. It was at least the ghost of something that he had experienced before.

Except then her mouth met his, freshly scented with the words she had just spoken, and it was as if he had never been kissed before in his life.

As if she had found a way to weave the words into every pass of her mouth over his. And he was undone.

There before a crowd of people. He, Gunnar Magnusson, who had never once been undone.

Who was the undoing and ruin of many, but had never been touched by another soul.

And when it was through, the crowd cheered, and Olive put one arm in the air, and laughed, and he knew that the photos that were being taken made it look for all the world like she was a joyous bride.

There would be interviews, and they would do them. They had already agreed. It was not his favorite thing to do, but Olive was a PR machine, and she wanted to give a story, though they had told all media outlets that they would not be speaking until after the wedding, since they would be far too busy preparing to devote any time to media.

It had been true, more or less.

For all that they were doing this wedding, they were still bound to each other. And in the meantime, he was in the process of making sure that the acquisition of Ambient remained legal, and did not in fact violate antitrust laws. But it was beginning to disquiet his spirit.

He had wanted revenge on her, or so he'd told himself.

He was beginning to wonder if what he'd really wanted was her.

And now there was a farcical reception to get through, and what he wanted was to be alone with her.

What he wanted was to claim her.

That echoed through his body with ever increasing insistence as they socialized, ate cake and pretended to be amused by the shocked commentary of their guests regarding the change in their relationship.

But what it really was, was a slow burn. A smolder, a promise of what was to come.

He had a surprise for her.

Because what he had wanted, truly, was an opportunity to have her alone. To have her to himself.

They would be going back to Iceland.

And they would be spending three days in his bed, doing nothing else. He had meals prepared, and very few clothes. He would get this intense need for her out of his system. And then, things would go back to the way they had been. Because this meant nothing to him, this wedding, the first wedding he had ever been to, which happened to be his own. And she meant nothing to him. It was easy to feel a sense of affection for Olive, but that was part of who she was.

She engendered that response in everybody, he could see it here.

That she also brought it out in him was not a surprise.

And when it was done, the private jet was waiting, and he picked her up, and carried her aboard.

She was his wife now.

And suddenly, it felt altogether different.

When they arrived at the house in Iceland, everything had been positioned just so. And the table was set with a romantic dinner for the two of them.

"This is beautiful," she said.

"Yes," he agreed.

He had not noticed until she had turned away from him at the wedding, but her gown had no back.

The torment of all that bare skin when he'd had to behave himself had been… It had been impossible.

What was it about her that bewitched him so?

She was brilliant, he knew that. But he had never felt compelled to take lovers that matched his mind.

For they filled a space in his bed, and nothing more. He did not need to make conversation with them. They existed only to slake generalized lust that he felt. But the desire that Olive created in him was specific.

And it was more than sex. It was tangled up with hearth smoke and warmth, and it made him want to push it away. Made him want to deny it. But she was having his child, and perhaps that was it.

A child.

And he was bringing that child into a union that he enforced.

A union that saw him taking over the company that mattered so much to all of them.

She had explained why. Exhaustively. Also why she was willing to let it go. To try something new.

Olive seemed to turn over her own motivations endlessly. The motivations of others.

And when she spoke of them, she made him understand. In a way he had never even understood himself.

He wanted only to strip her naked now. Forget dinner.

Because all of this overthinking was beginning to get to him, and he did not have any patience for it.

"I believe we can take our dinner later," he said.

He pulled her up against him, pressing his hands flat to her bare back.

She felt like heaven. Like silk and cream and uniquely his Olive. "Little Olive," he said, biting her lower lip. She gasped, rolling her body against him in that particular way she did. He loved that about her. It was not a move born out of experience, but rather she simply did what seemed to feel good to her. And she did it with abandon.

She did it out of desire.

It soothed something in him. To know that she was as caught up in all of this as he was.

"You like my dress?" she whispered.

"It is distracting as hell," he said. "And don't think I didn't notice that it's your preferred style."

Her entire face lit up. She laughed. And she looked at him like no one else ever had. "You noticed," she said. "That delights me. I love that you noticed. I thought that you would find it both amusing, and be slightly relieved that I didn't wear black."

"I'm surprised that you didn't."

"I wanted to dress for you. I wanted you to think that I was beautiful."

And that took all of it and turned what had just happened on its head.

Maybe she wasn't telling the truth. Maybe. Because he had been convinced that it was a performance for those who had been in attendance, but she claimed that it was for him.

That she had wanted him to think she was beautiful. But why would that matter?

"Of course I think you're beautiful. The problem is, I think you are beautiful, even when you wear your black turtlenecks. I may not like them, but I am powerless against the desire that you create in my body, whatever you have on. Or off."

She flushed with pleasure, and he was pleased for having been the one to create the response in her. Such a unique little Olive. Singular and bright. And his. Irrevocably his.

He moved his hands over her body, over the bare skin on her back, and it was not food he was hungry for. Not when he held Olive in his arms.

He kissed her, all that sweetness, and he had to look away when she stared up with those beautiful eyes.

He knew what it was to be on the receiving end of her ire. But this adoration that glowed there, it was foreign. And strange.

He had to turn away from it. He had to close the distance between them and claim her sweet, soft mouth. He kissed her, claimed her. Because that was what his blood demanded that he do. Because that was what made all of this feel real.

For he had married this woman today, making vows that he had never intended to make, facing the future he had never intended to have. Or rather, one he had never truly thought of. It was one thing to think that perhaps someday he might have a child. And that the child might inherit his company. But it was another thing of having a child with Olive, to know what she knew about growing up in the environment they had.

To be offering her the exact same thing for the baby that she carried. It felt wrong. In a way that he could never have anticipated.

And so he kissed her, because that was something he knew how to do. He knew how to pleasure her. He knew how to touch her. How to kiss her. He knew how to light the match that would ignite them both.

His skin burned with her touch, but at his core, he remained ice.

She moved her hands over his chest, down to his stomach.

She kissed him like he was everything. Like they were everything.

She was bolder now, which seemed surprising, since she had been quite the forward little thing even the first time. But now she touched him with the familiarity of what was being built between them.

Like she knew just how to set him on fire.

And she did.

And it was a strange thing, the sudden urgency that gripped him, to make love to his bride.

His bride.

And this was the old ways, the old sense of possession, of having. That was what overtook him now.

He stripped his clothes off, as quickly as possible, and naked, carried her into the bedroom.

She clung to his shoulders, her lips parted, her eyes wide with pleasure.

There were furs on his bed, plush and soft, and he

laid her down there and looked his fill. He wanted to see her naked. Of course he did. But it was not what he wanted most of all. Not now.

What he wanted most of all was to have her in that gown.

He moved his hands down to where the fabric skimmed her ankles and pushed it up past her knees, up to her waist, exposing the white lace panties she wore beneath. He moved his fingertips over that flimsy fabric. And watched as her hips jerked up off of the bed.

Watched as she lost herself in the rhythm of his touch, as he devoted himself only to her pleasure. He slipped his fingertips beneath the elastic there, touched her, moved his hands over her wetness, found her slick and ready and desirable for him.

She flexed her hips along with the movement, and he thrust two fingers deep into her, glorying in that silken desire.

He pulled her panties off, leaving her bare, spread her legs wide and looked his fill. In that wedding dress. White and for him. Only him.

A virgin. His virgin bride—though she may not be a virgin now, she had been when he had taken her, and it stoked a beastly fire in him, spoke to the savage at his core that he had not fully realized existed.

That she carried his baby.

It was a thunderous instinct. A wild demand. A testosterone-fueled fury.

His woman. His. His child.

All of the things that he had sworn that he didn't want. That he had sworn he would never take for his own.

And somewhere in the center of it was that little house. That little house with smoke coming out of the chimney, surrounded by snow. This was heat, but at its center was warmth, and they were two very different things. And it was the warmth that he denied. The warmth that he pushed away as he allowed himself to be swallowed whole by the flame.

He kissed her thigh, and then her very center, meeting his fill as he embraced the intensity of his arousal. As he lost himself in the pounding, swirling, never-ending need.

Oh, but how he wanted this woman.

Most of all.

He wanted to claim her profoundly. Wanted to be skin to skin, and yet, he would deny himself that now.

Because this was his moment to have his wife on their wedding day, in that glorious symbol of her purity, while he brought her down to the depths with him. She was not an angel. She was better than that. Sharp, determined, brilliant. And his.

This intoxicating, seemingly incompatible mix of things that electrified his soul.

There was nothing easy about this, and he had to laugh at what she had said about human nature. People would always want the easy thing. But this... This threatened to peel his skin from his bones. To carve him into something entirely new.

He rose up onto his knees, and fisted his arousal, bringing it to the slick part of her, and driving home.

She arched up off the bed, her silk-covered breasts heaving with the force of her desire.

He gripped her hips and pumped into her hard, fast, running away from something. Some demon, some unimaginable force that felt like it was chasing after him as the hounds of hell.

And it would catch him. Consume him.

It would destroy him. Bring him low.

And yet, it was quite possibly the only thing that would ever allow him to breathe.

In her he had found his destruction, and his renewal, and there was not a clear path ahead of him.

Except that she was his. His.

She cried out, her internal muscles pulsing around him as her orgasm overtook her, and he followed behind, roaring as if it were a great victory in battle, crying out his claiming as if there were ears to hear.

And then it was over. The storm. And yet it simply felt like the quiet of it. Not the end. Not truly. For it was only the beginning. She curled up against him, nestled in the furs, her head on his chest.

And he could see their lives entwined, bringing them to this moment, and yet, even seeing it all, it made no sense. How had they arrived here?

Inevitable winds of fate? He did not believe in such things. A man made his own path.

And yet she felt like something more than a choice.

"I'm hungry," she said softly.

And when they ate dinner, they did so naked, wrapped in furs, with her looking delightfully disheveled.

They spent the next few days like that. There was no reason to wear clothes. There was no contact with the outside world. It was simply the two of them, lost in a reality that could not be contained outside of this place.

For a media frenzy awaited them, and the demand to perform. And none of that was here. Here, there was nothing but their bodies. Nothing but their pleasure. Here, he began to feel something like comfort. Something like home.

And it felt like something close to peace for the first time since he had left the one place he had ever truly thought of as home.

Olive was beginning to realize that nothing was going to magically spark between the two of them that would prevent her from having a conversation she simply didn't want to have.

She was beginning to realize that it was different when you had your actual emotions invested in something. It wasn't going to be clean or easy or quick. It wasn't just a business deal. It did matter how it happened. It mattered… All of it.

The things that she had done before had been out of allegiance to her father. A desire to give him exactly what he wanted, even though he wasn't here. But this was for her.

Her feelings for Gunnar were hers.

And the risk was hers.

It was such a catastrophic feeling. She felt rocked,

altered. She felt afraid. Because she was going to have to risk something, not a contract. Her soul.

But she had made a decision.

He had bought her the skimpiest bathing suit of all time, as if a bathing suit were at all necessary here. But she wondered if he liked it purely for decoration. He did that sometimes. Make love to her with her clothes on. He had her naked too, but there seemed to be a particular thing he got out of leaving articles of clothing in place. She couldn't deny there was something sexy about it. When all he could manage to do was open the front of his pants and have her with all of his other items in place, it made her feel cherished, which was a funny thing, because she never would've imagined that animalistic passion could equate to feeling cherished, but it did. It made her feel special. Made her feel like she mattered.

Like she was something special to him.

She worried sometimes that she was simply a shackle. Because he had done this for the sake of their baby, and yet... They didn't talk about the baby. They didn't really... They didn't really speak of the future. It was difficult. Strange. This thing between them. It seemed wholly focused on them, and yet he would never have said that he was doing this because of her.

Or maybe he would. It was the asking, that was what she had to do.

"I have something a little bit different planned for tonight," she said.

What she had learned, being up there on the mountain, was that there were people she could call for assistance. And for the two hours a day that they were both off doing work, she had sacrificed a little bit of time planning this.

"You're going to want to bundle up," she said. "It's going to be cold."

She could have told him to bring his swimsuit, but she wanted him naked.

She wanted him to have absolutely no defenses at all when she did this.

It was dark, the northern lights visible out over the snow, green and purple and all the light. They cast beauty out onto the stark landscape, and it gave her hope.

Bundled in her parka, she took his hand in her mittened one, and began to lead him down the side of the mountain. She knew now where the path was that took them to the hot springs.

"What is this?" he asked when they arrived down there to a table set with food, and heaters placed around. "You have set us up food on the tundra."

"Yes," she said. "I have. I wished to take you on a date without entering into civilization. This seemed like a reasonable enough way to do it."

The dinner was exquisite, lamb, fish and potatoes.

Extremely Icelandic, and she could see by the look on Gunnar's face, that it tapped into something special.

She knew that this place was special to him. That no matter how much time he spent in the rest of the world, this was his home. His heart.

The scary thing was, this was an unforgiving, harsh, frozen landscape.

But there were also northern lights. There were miracles. Hot springs. Possibilities. And she had to hope that his heart reflected all those things in the same way as his homeland. She had to hope that that was true.

As soon as he finished eating she unzipped her coat, and revealed that she had nothing but a bikini top underneath.

His gaze suddenly became keen. Extremely interested.

"I had thought that we might use the hot springs."

"Indeed."

She shimmied out of her boots and pants, and stepped into the steaming, pale blue pool. He was not far behind her, stripping his clothes off, moving down into the pool and taking her into his arms.

He kissed her, her neck, on down her shoulder blades, making his way to her breasts, he clearly loved her breasts.

And she arched her back, rubbed her nipples against his hair-covered chest, gloried in the textural differences between them. In his strength.

But this was different than the other times they had come together. Those times had always been furious, intense. Growling and fighting, and she loved them.

But she wanted to show him something else. She wanted to show him her heart. And so, she swam away from him, to the corner of the pool. And he followed. But when he rejoined her, she wrapped her arms firmly around his neck, and kissed him. She made the kiss long and deep, keeping her hands firmly clasped behind his neck, preventing herself from exploring the rest of his hard, beautiful body, as much as she wanted to. And she poured everything into it. All the things that were hard for her to say. All the things that she felt with every last bit of her heart.

Finally, she broke the kiss off, and began to move her hands over his muscles, and as if he sensed that this was her moment, something she must do, he kept his hands at his sides, and allowed her unfettered access to his body.

She explored the planes of his chest, the glorious ripples in his stomach. She moved her hands to his thighs. He had a warrior's body. And that, she realized, he was. Fighting an endless battle to find victory.

But she wondered what he was trying to claim victory against. For all that they had been together, she had not been able to entice him to share.

And tonight, she realized she could not kick the ice wall down. She had to melt it.

It was all that could be done.

With an elegant lift of her body beneath the water, she brought herself down over his stiff arousal, lowering herself slowly onto his shaft. She clung to his shoulders as she took him into her body, as she reveled in this moment. She looked up, dizzy, the light swirling above, mingling with those crushed glitter stars, doing their best to light up a black velvet night.

It was them. All that velvet darkness, and never-ending hope.

Hope.

She hoped for better without even ever seeing it with her own eyes. She hoped for more for the two of them without any assurance that such a thing existed. Without a certainty that it was possible.

It was faith, at the end of the day, something she had never put a lot of thought into. But that was love. Faith, hope and love were all part of the same thing. You could not have one without desperately wanting another. Without clinging as hard as possible to another.

For this love in her heart was the substance of all that was hoped for, and she took her peace in the fact that she knew she did not have to see it for it to be there.

Love.

Oh, how she loved him.

As her body began to quake with pleasure, as she began to shatter in his arms, she whispered those words.

The words that she had been too afraid to speak all this time. "I love you."

He growled, his climax overtaking him, and she felt his surrender, and for just that moment, she let it shine within her like lights in the northern sky.

I love you.

No. This could not be borne. This could not be.

I love you.

It brought back with scalding clarity words within

him that he had not thought of for years. Words that no one had said to him in so long…

I love you.

He gritted his teeth. "Let us go back to the house," he said.

"Is that all you have to say?"

"It is all there is to be said."

"That isn't true. And you know that. I said that I loved you, Gunnar, and now you're telling me you want to go back to the house. The appropriate answer is to either say that you love me in return, or tell me that you don't, but acting like the words were never spoken feels a bit like a lie."

"In all things, I have never been a liar. That is you."

"Well, that suits your narrative right now, doesn't it? That somehow what I have to say to you isn't true. But I love you. And you are being a coward."

"I don't love, I told you that."

"Why. Why? Look, I know what it's like to be hurt by the person who's supposed to love you, but during this time, these past couple months, I've been rebuilding myself. And with that, came the realization that the company isn't the most important thing to me. Not anymore. I don't want to raise our child in an environment where love is conditional. Where performance is the only thing that matters. I can't deal with that. Live like that. I want love. I've never been loved before. Not really. And I want a life, a house, a world that is filled with love. I don't think that's wrong. Is it wrong? I would hope that it's not. I would hope that it is entirely understandable that what I want is… What I want is to be cared for. But I've done all this work to break down the barriers in my soul, and I want you to do it too. I wanted to come out here. Because I know this is your heart. I want you to tell me. I want you to tell me."

"Enough," he said.

"No. I'm not going to be afraid. You married me. You're stuck with me. What are you going to do? Stay married to me for a week? Deny me, divorce me, just because I'm not doing everything that you want? I don't think that is a very reasonable move. I simply don't. So, here's what I think. I'm going to push. Because that's who I am. But you know what else… Love isn't a contract negotiation. There isn't a winner and a loser. And there are no prizes for a grudging acceptance. I want you to love me. I want you to love me because you have no other choice."

"Let me tell you what you don't know about my life," he said. "Until I was twelve I was raised here. I never left Iceland. I never left the country. I never knew my mother, she left when I was a baby. But I lived with my grandparents. Her parents. We lived in a small house out in the middle of nowhere. I spent all my days in the snow. In the wilderness. I would come home to warm dinner, and people who were there for me. Who cared. They taught me to love this land. They taught me what mattered. But I was enamored of a man who had never even come to visit me. Enamored of his money, his power. He took me and he tried to…

to bend me into his image. To break me into it. Before he died, I told him that he had failed." And suddenly, his soul felt as cold as the world around him. "But he didn't. He stripped something from me that I will never be able to get back. He stole the only warmth, the only love that I ever knew."

He thought of when he'd tried to go back. He thought of it, but he could not bring himself to walk through the memory. Not now.

"Gunnar," she said. "I want that house that you're talking about. I want that love. I want to be that thing for our child. I want simple and beautiful and ours. I want it to be home. I want it to be filled with love. Your father didn't win unless you allow him to. A man chooses his own steps. I know that you believe that. You took what your grandparents taught you, and you made your company focus on the planet. Because you loved the wilderness that you grew up in. Because you took that love and you carried it out with you. It isn't gone. It had to take a different shape."

"You don't know, Olive," he said. "It does not matter. This. We have passion. And that is enough."

She shook her head. "It matters to me. It matters to me, and I cannot live in a place where I am not loved. Not again. Not ever again. Gunnar, I want our life to be different. Wholly different. I want it to be everything that we could've ever dreamed of. When we were children, when we believed everything was possible. Not now. Not as cynical adults, taking what we've been told we're allowed.

"No. What I want is a miracle. And I don't see why we can't have it."

"Because there are no miracles left in this world."

He thought of the empty cabin.

The pipe, sitting cold on the counter.

Never to be smoked again.

Two people who were gone, with Gunnar never having a chance to see them again. To say that he was sorry.

"Look at the sky," Olive said. "If that's not a miracle, then what is? Look at us. If we are not a miracle… I don't know what is."

"There are no miracles in this life. That is just science. And we're just two people who had sex, and are now dealing with the consequences."

And he could see the moment that he had lost her. And it was a moment that he knew true terror. Because he had not imagined that he could lose her. He had thought… He had thought that she would stay.

"But I love you," she said. "I love you, and I want you to love me. Why can't you trust that? Why can't you trust me?"

"Olive, I trust nothing. Nothing. I was a boy, who grew up in the safest, most loving home possible, and what did I want? More. More. I was greedy. I looked at my father, I saw his wealth and his success and I thought… I thought it would be happier with him? And for what? Because I was blinded by the trappings of all that he had, and I could not have been more wrong. And if I could be wrong about him…"

"It's why you were so angry with me, isn't it? Because you believed better about me, and I proved you wrong. And I'm sorry. I'm so sorry. But you have to understand. It didn't come from a place of wanting to hurt you. I was just trying to do what my father wanted."

"Enough. I don't care about that. Not anymore."

"You are afraid that you can't trust your judgment, and I only made that worse. I only…"

"It is not you, you fool. It is me. I do not trust myself."

"Gunnar…"

"That is the way of it. The truth of it, Olive. I *chose* to leave them. I betrayed them. I squandered the love that I had. I was a bad judge of character… But most of all… It is my own character that I have no certainty in. Because I looked around that cabin, I looked around at this frozen wasteland, and I did not love it. I did not esteem it. I wanted to go and live with my rich father. As if money might insulate me. As if money would make me happier. I knew nothing. And I will never be so complacent that I think that might've changed. Yes, I pride myself on my moral integrity that is only because I have written rules for myself that I will not compromise. I had love. And I squandered it for the shallow things in life."

"You were a boy."

"A boy who broke the hearts of the only two people who ever loved him. A boy who left them to die alone. My grandfather went first. And then my grandmother… And who was there with her, Olive? Because it was not me. Those hands that held mine when I learned to walk. Those hands that taught me to fish, taught me to cook. They were empty when she died, because I was not there. How can I ever speak of love. I had it and I squandered it. I failed when he came to get me. I had a little wooden soldier in my hand. He took it from me, and looked at it. He said that I should leave it because I could have much better with him. And so I left it. And it is… It is the one thing that you cannot get back, Olive. The simple things that you squander, thinking that you will replace them with money. You won't. You can't."

"So take this. Take it now. I can't replace what you lost, but I am here. I'm here."

"My heart was turned to stone long ago. It cannot be fixed. Not now."

"Gunnar please," she said, the words raw.

"There is nothing to be done, little Olive."

She looked bleak, cold and tired. And then, she turned her face up to him, and the stark sadness in her eyes gutted him.

"I will be setting up residence somewhere else," she said. "I will stay married to you. I will allow you full visitation of our child. As much as you like. But I need to be free. I need to be free to live my life. To feel loved. I cannot exchange one man in my life with expectations on me that come from a place that has nothing to do with how much he cares, for another. I'm sorry, Gunnar. But that's how it has to be."

"No," he said, his voice rough, the denial bursting from him.

"I'm sorry," she said. "I can't do this. I can't. I lived my whole life with a man who wanted me around only for what he could train me to be. How are you different? How are we different?"

He felt as if he was being wrenched in two.

He watched as she got out of the pool. As she dried herself and dressed herself. An entirely different woman to the one that he had brought here first.

This one would not shrink against the wind.

And she did not shrink against him.

And he had no idea what the hell he was supposed to do with that.

Go after her.

And yet, he stood frozen. As Olive hiked back up the mountain. As she took that torn piece of him with her. And it felt like a terrible metaphor. Because Olive was strong enough to hike up the mountain, and he stood frozen, in the pain of his past.

And suddenly, it was as if the frozen ice blocks inside of him began to crack. Crumble.

And he wanted to roar at the sky.

Because he had only ever loved his grandparents, and he had lost them. And then he had spent a childhood being abused by a man who hadn't loved him at all.

But Olive… Maybe it was because Olive had never known the warmth of home, that she didn't fear its loss. Because she didn't know what it was like to return to an empty cabin and find out that the people in it had died years ago.

And you would never have the chance to say good-bye.

He dressed, and he called his pilot.

There was something he needed to do. Somewhere he needed to go.

He was a man who had been all around the world, but there was one last journey he had to take.

CHAPTER SIXTEEN

OLIVE WAS WRETCHED. But she was the one who had decided to go back to the States. She began to work at making arrangements for where she might go and be with her baby.

She began to think in earnest about what kind of life she would build. What kind of mother she would be.

It all started her thinking about who she was in a way she never had before.

She was resourceful, and resilient, she wanted to be soft. She had always been trained to be afraid to be. She didn't like to ask for help, and right now it felt as if she needed a lot of help. But maybe that was better. Maybe it was training.

Because she needed to embrace some of the vulnerability inside of her so that she could soften for a baby.

She started to write a letter, one that had nothing to do with press releases or the media. One that simply felt good. A list of promises. Ones that she was determined to keep.

And she did her best not to dissolve.

But what if you did?

It was a profound question. And it was one that sent a crack down to the very depths of her soul.

What if she did?

And so she wept. Openly. With her whole body.

She wept for the little girl she'd been. Who had spent her childhood waiting outside of boardrooms. Who had been angry at Gunnar for eating her cupcake, but not at her father for giving her a birthday party where the only semblance of a treat was a cupcake that just happened to be there, not even for her specifically. One that didn't make her special. One that didn't matter at all.

She wept for her childhood. For her teenage years. For the fact that she had taken everything seriously all this time.

For the fact that Gunnar was the person she loved so very much, when what she wanted was something normal.

And she did not think they could ever have that.

She wept for so many things. And she didn't feel weaker for it. Instead, she felt like she had found something new.

She was only very sorry that she had had to break her own heart to find it.

The helicopter pilot touched down in the snowfield, and Gunnar stepped out, standing before the darkened home.

He had bought it some years ago. Just to ensure that it stayed there.

He walked across the bleak, empty snowfield and pushed open the door.

It was impossibly cold, the fire in the hearth dead for these many years.

It was strange to see the place without so much as an ember.

The pipe was still there.

He walked over and touched it.

He wasn't sure why he had left it the first time. Why he hadn't kept it for himself.

Really, it did not make sense.

And yet, if he thought of it truthfully, it did. He had spent all these years running away from how much this place hurt.

He walked into the back bedroom, where the quilt his grandmother had made was still spread over the bed.

This was the only place where he had experienced love.

A love he hadn't deserved.

A love he had squandered.

And now he had the offer of love again, the offer of a life, from Olive.

How could he accept her love? How? He was wrong about all these sorts of things. He'd had love. He had love and he had squandered it. He had seen something shinier, something that he thought was better. And he had been wrong. So desperately wrong. He had stolen from himself a life of warmth and love and simplicity. And he had exchanged it for fists of fury and barren rooms. He had exchanged it for years where he had lived with a man who had done his level best to strip the humanity from him, and he had to fight for all that he was to cling to it. To cling to that cabin. To cling to its warmth. To remember that when his temper had flared his grandfather had taught him ways to cope with it. That his grandmother had showed him softness.

He had betrayed them. The cost had been everything. Everything. And they died. They died and he had never been back. How could he accept love now? How?

Knowing what he had squandered… Knowing how…

How little he could trust his own heart.

Perhaps he needed to trust hers.

Because he had been given love once. And it had been keen and clear and bright. And it was the same sort of love that he had seen reflected in Olive's face.

His Olive. They were like nothing. He'd said that to her. And it was true.

If that's not a miracle, then what is? Look at us. If we are not a miracle… I don't know what is.

He had thought those feelings long dead in him. And he had thrown the issue of her betrayal in front of them, because it was easy. Because it was easy to tap into that old fury, that old hurt at the way he had been wrong about his father.

Far easier than admitting…

Of course he had always loved her. Of course. She was everything to him, and she had been for all this time. He had thought, not so long ago, that if he had been another man he might've loved her. But he always had.

He had just been desperate not to label it thus, because part of him knew…

If he wanted love, then he had to reckon with his

past. If he wanted love, Olive was right. He had to let it go. To keep what warmed him, and to set aside what hurt him.

She had always been there. The only good thing. The only healing thing. Waiting to be ready. Waiting for him to be ready.

They were more than a miracle. They were fate. But fate was not going to chase him down.

He was going to have to do some work. No matter how hard it might be.

"I'm sorry," he said, his breath coming out in a fog, the apology lingering in the air. "I am so sorry I left you. I didn't know. I didn't understand."

He was bringing a child into this world. And perhaps that meant…perhaps that meant finding forgiveness for the boy he'd been.

The boy who had walked away from this and into a life of cold manipulation that had made him desperately unhappy.

His sin had been trust.

His sin had been loving someone undeserving of it.

Was that so unforgivable? Could he not release it?

And he suddenly knew, that he could not give his child the life he wanted without risking himself. He could not have Olive without risking himself. She was a bright, beautiful woman who showed him continually that she was his match in every way, and he was lowering himself: He was not giving her all that he could.

And he was doing it out of fear. He wanted to prove that he was the best, he had acted as if that put him above her. That he would not cheat on something like a project. But the truth of it was, Olive had been willing to compromise everything for the love of her father. Olive had been willing to risk herself to tell him that she loved him. And he hadn't risked a damn thing for her. Olive was the brave one. She was the one that was honest.

He did not deserve her. He was not worthy of her. And suddenly, like a light in the darkness, he knew the truth.

It shone into the very depths of his soul, and kept him from being able to lie. To himself, to anyone else.

He had loved Olive for a very long time. It was only his cowardice that kept him from admitting it was so. And if he wanted to be half the man that she was a woman, he had to change everything now.

What good was being a man forged in the fires, a man whose blood cried out for battle if he could not fight for the one thing that mattered.

No matter the cost.

She was wretched. She had cried herself hoarse, and then gone to sleep in their bed.

Well, it had been their bed. What it would be next would be determined by what she did.

And she was waiting. Waiting for him to return. Waiting to see what her life would look like. She would have her child. So there was that. She had to cling to that.

"I am prepared to do this," she said.

She stood up, and when she turned around, he was standing there. In the doorway, his eyes ice blue. And something in her shifted. She felt as if they were standing in a boardroom, ready and able to have the biggest negotiation of their life.

"I cannot stay if you don't love me."

"You can't, or you won't?"

"I'm no longer willing to sacrifice myself to the needs of others. I will not do it. I want to be loved. And yes, I want all of this for my child, but I want it for myself as well. I need it for myself. I need to have this."

"I am willing," he said.

And he said it as if it was a forfeited business. And her whole heart turned to stone.

"You see, I have focused on winning to make what I did worthwhile. Leaving my grandparents for as long as I did. I could've come back, much earlier than I did. Much, much earlier. But I didn't, out of fear. I stayed away, and I kept working hard, and when I returned, they had… They had died. I waited too long. And so his success became everything. I never wanted to experience loss again. Ever. I could not face it. But what is the point of living if we are not trying, in all of our messy glory, to love? What is the purpose of it?"

"I don't know," she said.

"Neither do I. Not anymore. Not now. For I have ascended to the heights professionally, I could've had my revenge on you, but none of it fixed who I am, what I was. Nothing has come close to fixing anything. But when I was with you in the hot springs, beneath the northern lights, I could nearly believe it. In miracles. In love. In a little house out in the country."

"I love you," she said.

And she ran forward, closing the distance between them, and kissing him on the mouth.

"I need to show you something," he whispered against her lips.

"I'll follow you anywhere." She smiled. "Or you know, you could kidnap me."

"Kidnap?"

"A little pillaging, a little ravishing…"

"Later, my love, later."

Shortly after that, Olive found herself on a plane, bound for Iceland.

The cabin Gunnar brought her to was his home, she knew it, without him having to tell her.

"Oh, Gunnar…"

She walked through the little place, looking at the hand carved furniture. At the small, remaining signs of the lives that had once been here.

And then she saw something, just very small, beneath one of the little beds.

She bent down and discovered a small, wooden soldier.

"Gunnar."

She turned and he was standing in the doorway.

"I found this."

"Olive…"

"It's been here all along. Waiting for you." She looked up at him, and she smiled. "It was waiting for you to find your way home."

He took her in his arms, his voice low and fierce. "Yes, that may be true. But first… Olive first, I had to find you."

"I was there the whole time."

He kissed her then, deep and hard. "Yes, you were. You were."

"I love you."

"I love you too."

There must be, Olive thought, a German word for that unbearable feeling of caring for someone so very much you thought you might break apart. And then she realized, there were no words for it. There was only this. Only two hearts that had long stood divided on opposite sides of the boardroom, that had become one over time, and would stay one, because of the miracle of love.

EPILOGUE

IT WAS CHRISTMAS, their favorite time of year. Snow fell outside, and everybody was tucked up in their little beds, beneath handmade quilts. The fire was going, and he knew from experience that smoke from the small stovepipe chimney was pouring into the frigid air.

The cabin was their Christmas tradition.

And they all loved it. Including the kids.

It was smaller than their other homes throughout the world, but it would always be the most special home. The most real.

He and Olive did not work so much these days. Delegating various tasks to other people of the company. What Olive had decided to do was not start a company at all. She had started writing children's books. Her particular brand of ridiculous humor in banter creating a series of exceedingly popular works. About a young girl who had to spend her days in office buildings while her dad had meetings, and the different shenanigans she got up to.

But he would've loved her whatever she did, because she was his.

Because she had given him his home back.

He looked at the Christmas tree in the corner, and the sleeping children in their beds.

She had given him his heart back.

* * * * *

Shocked by the drama in
The Billionaire's Baby Negotiation*?*
Then make sure you don't miss out on these other
Millie Adams stories!

The Scandal Behind the Italian's Wedding
Stealing the Promised Princess
Crowning His Innocent Assistant
The Only King to Claim Her
His Secretly Pregnant Cinderella

Available now!

#4033 THE SECRET THAT SHOCKED CINDERELLA
by Maisey Yates
Riot wakes from a coma with no recollection of Kravann, the brooding fiancé at her bedside, *or* her baby! Her amnesia has given Kravann a second chance. Can he get their whirlwind love affair right this time?

#4034 EMERGENCY MARRIAGE TO THE GREEK
by Clare Connelly
Tessa returns to billionaire Alexandros's life with an outrageous emergency request—for his ring! But if he's going to consider her proposal, he has some conditions of his own: a *real* marriage...and an heir!

#4035 STOLEN FOR MY SPANISH SCANDAL
Rival Billionaire Tycoons
by Jackie Ashenden
My reunion with my stepbrother Constantine Silvera resulted in an explosion of forbidden, utterly unforgettable passion...leaving me pregnant! The Spaniard is determined to claim our child. So now here I am, unceremoniously kidnapped and stranded in his beautiful manor house!

#4036 WILLED TO WED HIM
by Caitlin Crews
To save her family legacy, her father's will demands that Annika wed superrich yet intimidating Ranieri. She knows he's marrying her in cold blood, but behind the doors of his Manhattan penthouse, he ignites a fire in her she never dreamed possible...

HPCNMRA0722

#4037 INNOCENT UNTIL HIS FORBIDDEN TOUCH
Scandalous Sicilian Cinderellas
by Carol Marinelli
PR pro Beatrice's brief is simple—clean up playboy prince Julius's image before he becomes king. A challenge made complicated by the heat she feels for her off-limits client! For the first time, innocent Beatrice *wants* to give in to wild temptation...

#4038 THE DESERT KING MEETS HIS MATCH
by Annie West
Sheikh Salim needs a wife—immediately! But when he's introduced to matchmaker Rosanna, he's hit with a red-hot jolt of recognition... Because she's the fiery stranger from an electric encounter he *never* forgot!

#4039 CLAIMED TO SAVE HIS CROWN
The Royals of Svardia
by Pippa Roscoe
After lady-in-waiting Henna stops a marriage that would protect King Aleks's throne, he's furious. Until a transformational kiss awakens him to a surprising new possibility that could save his crown... And it starts with *her*!

#4040 THE POWERFUL BOSS SHE CRAVES
Scandals of the Le Roux Wedding
by Joss Wood
Event planner Ella is done with men who call the shots. So when commanding Micah requests her expertise for his sister's society wedding, she can't believe she's considering it. Only there's something about her steel-edged new boss that intrigues and attracts Ella beyond reason...

YOU CAN FIND MORE INFORMATION ON UPCOMING HARLEQUIN TITLES, FREE EXCERPTS AND MORE AT HARLEQUIN.COM.

HPCNMRB0722

SPECIAL EXCERPT FROM

⟨H⟩ **HARLEQUIN**
PRESENTS

*My reunion with my stepbrother Constantin Silvera
resulted in an explosion of forbidden, utterly
unforgettable passion...leaving me pregnant! The
Spaniard is determined to claim our child. So now
here I am, unceremoniously kidnapped and stranded
in his beautiful manor house!*

*Read on for a sneak preview of
Jackie Ashenden's next story for Harlequin Presents*
Stolen for My Spanish Scandal

Constantin's black winged brows drew down very
slightly. "So, you haven't come here to tell me?"

Cold swept through me, my gut twisting and making
me feel even more ill. I put a hand on the back of the
uncomfortable couch, steadying myself, because he
couldn't know. He couldn't. I'd told no one. It was my
perfect little secret and that was how I'd wanted it to
stay.

"Tell you?" I tried to sound as innocent as possible,
to let my expression show nothing but polite inquiry.

"Tell you what?"

His inky brows twitched as he looked down at me from his great height, his beautiful face as expressive as a mountainside. "That you're pregnant, of course."

Don't miss
Stolen for My Spanish Scandal,
available September 2022 wherever
Harlequin Presents books and ebooks are sold.

Harlequin.com

Get 4 FREE REWARDS!

We'll send you 2 FREE Books <u>plus</u> 2 FREE Mystery Gifts.

FREE
Value Over
$20

Both the **Harlequin® Desire** and **Harlequin Presents®** series feature compelling novels filled with passion, sensuality and intriguing scandals.

YES! Please send me 2 FREE novels from the Harlequin Desire or Harlequin Presents series and my 2 FREE gifts (gifts are worth about $10 retail). After receiving them, if I don't wish to receive any more books, I can return the shipping statement marked "cancel." If I don't cancel, I will receive 6 brand-new Harlequin Presents Larger-Print books every month and be billed just $5.80 each in the U.S. or $5.99 each in Canada, a savings of at least 11% off the cover price or 6 Harlequin Desire books every month and be billed just $4.55 each in the U.S. or $5.24 each in Canada, a savings of at least 13% off the cover price. It's quite a bargain! Shipping and handling is just 50¢ per book in the U.S. and $1.25 per book in Canada.* I understand that accepting the 2 free books and gifts places me under no obligation to buy anything. I can always return a shipment and cancel at any time. The free books and gifts are mine to keep no matter what I decide.

Choose one: ☐ **Harlequin Desire**
(225/326 HDN GNND)

☐ **Harlequin Presents Larger-Print**
(176/376 HDN GNWY)

Name (please print)

Address   Apt. #

City   State/Province   Zip/Postal Code

Email: Please check this box ☐ if you would like to receive newsletters and promotional emails from Harlequin Enterprises ULC and its affiliates. You can unsubscribe anytime.

HARLEQUIN

Heartfelt or thrilling, passionate or uplifting—Harlequin is more than just happily-ever-after.

With twelve different series to choose from and new books available every month, you are sure to find stories that will move you, uplift you, inspire and delight you.

HNEWS2021